THE FAIRY
TALE MUSEUM

SUSANNAH M. SMITH

THE FAIRY TALE MUSEUM

SUSANNAH M. SMITH

Invisible Publishing
Halifax & Picton

Library and Archives Canada Cataloguing in Publication

Smith, Susannah M., 1967-, author
    The fairy tale museum / Susannah M. Smith.

Issued in print and electronic formats.
ISBN 978-1-988784-06-9 (softcover).--ISBN 978-1-988784-07-6 (EPUB)

    I. Title.

PS8587.M593F35 2018   C813'.6   C2018-901097-5
                                               C2018-901098-3

Edited by Leigh Nash
Cover and interior design by Megan Fildes | Typeset in Laurentian
With thanks to type designer Rod McDonald

Printed and bound in Canada

Invisible Publishing | Halifax & Picton
www.invisiblepublishing.com

We acknowledge the support of the Canada Council for the Arts, which last year invested $20.1 million in writing and publishing throughout Canada.

Canada Council   Conseil des Arts
for the Arts   du Canada

A book can be almost anything. It can be a piece of paper you pleat like a fan with a single word written on every page. It can be an out-of-date guide book salvaged from the trash, remade by pasting into it images and passages snipped from old magazines. It can be a stack of lottery tickets and theatre tickets and numbered tickets from the meat counter at the store, hole-punched and gathered on a key ring. It can be three autumn leaves tied together with a piece of blue thread.

— LEAH HAGER COHEN

Everything is new. Everything is strange. Everything is possible.

— YUMI SAKUGAWA

EXHIBITION GUIDE

TABVLA CAP. X.

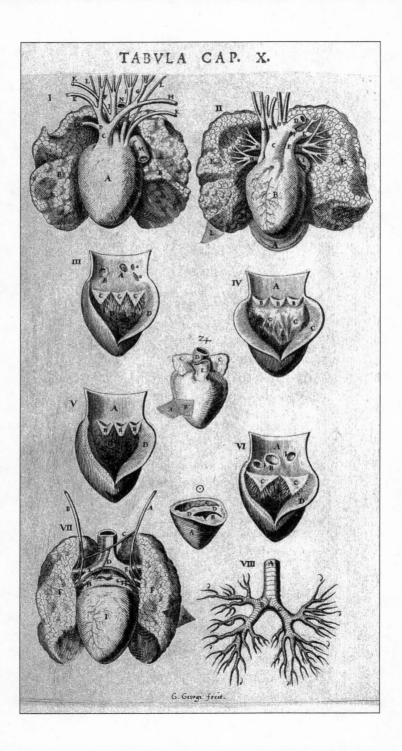

G. Georgi fecit.

INSTRUCTIONS FOR COLLECTORS

First, a confession.

I sometimes stay in the museum after hours. Sometimes I sleep there. You would think a museum would be quiet at night, but no. The objects talk to me. I have secret nooks where I listen. They tell me their stories while I make notes, scribbling in the dim light. Recording as much as I can. After all, as a curator, it is my job to listen and make connections.

Towards dawn, I often sneak home for a quick shower and a bowl of oatmeal. When I arrive back at the museum, crisp and clean and inspired, no one is any the wiser. I lay open my notes on my desk and survey the night's work. Few things are more pleasing than writing by hand in a notebook.

If I've learned one thing from the objects, it is this: the secret to life is loving what you do. Not in certain hours of certain days, but in every moment of every day. I have decided to love.

It was not always this way. Although I grew up in a family of collectors, there was a period of time when I stopped collecting. To be more accurate: I never stopped collecting completely, but I stopped believing in my collections. During that time, I felt adrift in the sea of the world, subject to random winds and tides and cut off from mystery and beauty, while happiness skirted my periphery. This continued for some time, until I finally realized that I had to take control of my own boat and come home to myself. So I chose a different course and resumed my observing, collecting, and documenting practice. I immediately regained a sense of purpose. Knowing what I now know, I will never lose my way in this manner again. You can't abandon your-self and expect to like your life.

And so, a short set of instructions.

1. Never allow someone else's no to annihilate your yes.

2. Always listen to and follow the thread of what attracts you, what ignites your curiosity. For example, the enchant-ment of drawers, the nesting of artifacts inside boxes, the joy of the secret wardrobe, the home inside the home inside the home—such delicious pleasures. Your yes is your guiding light.

3. Collect handmade images and objects. The value of the unique over the reproduction is inherent. Read Walter Benjamin—one of the great collectors—on this topic. The antique plate is always fully itself.

4. Your collection tells a story. In this collection, you can be anyone you want to be. You can create the story that matches who you are inside. You can change, you can trans-form, you can start again and again and again. This is the privilege of the collector.

5. Collecting equals learning. On many levels.

6. The object is a repository for magical thought. Objects contain stories. You have a relationship with the object. The object offers you its secrets. By association, you become magical.

7. Be ready to let everything go. The collection is meant to be shared. It starts its life with you and then you hand it over to other minds, other imaginations. In this way, the object becomes expansive and takes on a life of its own, carrying your contribution with it. Evolution is effortless and effervescent and never-ending. Always the forward momentum.

WUNDERKAMMER

THE MUSEUM

You approach the forest from the wooded path with the slant thrill of being among its eldritch creakings and shadows. Its vivid greens and abundance of decay and regrowth. Its hollow tree trunks and birds' nests. The countless secret hiding places.

A white fox appears at your side. The light filtering through the trees almost disappears as you venture further in. The air is alive with animals stirring. You imagine you can hear eyes blinking in the bracken. The fox is a steadfast ghost beside you. As you walk, the path disappears behind you, yet you feel compelled to continue. Your feet seem to know the way.

Hidden in the oldest trees at the heart of the forest is a castle. Like the fox, it appears ghostly. It is surrounded by a stone wall with two tiers of pointed railings and moss-covered pillars, each topped by an iron sphere.

You feel euphoric. Your body floats into the tree canopy. Up close, the leaves are layered, like scales. The towers crouch in the dark, lit up in places by lights in many tiny windows. As your eyes adjust, you begin to see gargoyles perched in nooks and under rooflines. Inside the mouth of one you see something glint. The moment you think, What is that? your hand is on its tongue.

You hold a golden key. Show me your door, you think, and you find yourself standing at the foot of the tallest tower. The key slides inside the lock that it was made for and the door swings open.

The room stretches so high you cannot see where it ends. Its walls are lined with shelves of books and ribboning flights of stairs. You start to climb the nearest staircase and pause at the first landing to run your hands along the spines of the books. You pull one off the shelf. The sound of ideas cascading over one another rushes instantly into your ears. You close the book. The sound stops. You put the book back on the shelf and choose another.

Open it.

Listen.

Close it.

Select another.

You continue in this way, walking up stairways and pausing on landings, opening books and letting torrents wash over you, until you come to a table. On it is a book with a cover that seems to shimmer. You pick it up. The golden key feels heavy in your pocket. Overcome with a wave of sleepiness, you slide to the floor. Your back is supported by shelves. You're so comfortable here. The place is quiet and peaceful. You open the book and close your eyes.

Your mind kaleidoscopes open. It is as if the book is a cabinet. It is as if the book contains drawer upon drawer of treasures and secret compartments that expand into passageways. Passageways that lead to rooms. Rooms that open up into worlds you have always dreamed of. Worlds within worlds. Your imagination unfurls.

You have entered the museum.

INTO THE WOODS

The story pieces have flown
up into the air

LITTLE BLACK RIDING HOOD

The weather has changed since her arrival. Fortunately, she'd had a vivid dream about storms the night before and thought to bring the wool cape her grandmother had made her.

She leaves the comfort of the house and makes her way down the path through the trees. A canvas bag on her back. A cool wind kicks up around her, lifting her hair. Dark clouds gather. She draws the black hood up over her head.

The chestnut trees drop their blossom petals like snow. They swirl in the air and collect in drifts beneath her feet. She strides forward, aware of the music the wind makes in the leaves and branches above her head.

She thinks of her grandmother's warm, weathered hands dipping wool in hot water to bind the fibres, and lifts her face into the wind. She smells rain. She walks a little faster, drawing the cape closer. How delicious, this gathering of energy, this being on the brink. How delicious, this feeling of something good about to happen, of knowing it's in the trees, it's coming.

THE WOLF, PART I

The wolf is imprisoned in a bell jar. He has stopped pacing and lies with his great shaggy head on his paws, occasionally opening his mouth to yawn. Waiting.

Shards of stories
are everywhere

BÖHMERWALD

Eros and Thanatos have escaped from *The Island of Doctor Moreau*. All those human-animal hybrids were getting to them. Now they're in the Bohemian Forest, standing on a bridge over the Moldau River, holding hands. Eros is flushed and glowing. A thin line of blood runs down Thanatos's jawbone. The river is loud. Eros hands him the ear trumpet.

Here. Where do you think we should go?

Thanatos inserts the tube in his ear and closes his eyes. He points.

That way. I hear civilization. It's not far off.

They cross the river and leave its roaring behind to follow a trail of moss-covered rocks.

Are you sure this is the way? Eros shifts his quiver across his back and looks at Thanatos sideways.

Thanatos nods, his pale face floating in the murk of the forest.

Don't fret. Stones have never failed me.

They pass peat bogs and trees damaged by acid rain. They keep walking, Thanatos with his eyes on the stones, Eros glancing around uneasily and breathing through his mouth. After a while, they reach a clearing in the trees. A stereopticon is set up to project images of buildings and spires onto the screen of the forest. A harmonium plays *La vie en rose*, its keys and bellows moving up and down, in and out.

We've reached the golden city, Eros says, blinking and pursing his mouth. Only, I wonder where the people are.

An owl in a tree above swivels its head and watches them. Thanatos looks up. There's blood on the bed of pine needles at their feet.

Is this mine? he asks.

Eros leans down, dips his finger in, and licks it. No. It's fresh, but it's not yours.

At the far end of the clearing a table is set with two places. Now the stereopticon projects images of food onto the trees.

I'm hungry, Eros says.

By the time they reach the table, it offers two crystal goblets filled with wine and a steaming roasted bird on a platter ringed with vegetables. They sit down and unfold the cloth napkins next to their plates. Thanatos puts his head in his hands and closes his eyes.

I'm tired, he says.

Eros takes a sip of wine and begins to carve the meat.

I'll fix you a plate.

I'm too tired to eat.

I'll feed you.

Eros shifts his chair to the other side of the table. He cuts the food into tiny pieces and spoons them one by one into Thanatos's mouth. Between bites he feeds himself and takes mouthfuls of wine. The harmonium is still playing Edith Piaf and the stereopticon has gone back to projecting images of a city. It shows a river spanned by stone bridges, street lamps, shops, and grand churches with stained glass.

Daylight in the forest is fading. A candelabrum materializes on the table, casting a small orange glow. Then, behind the blowing sound of the harmonium and the clink of cutlery on china, there is a low rustling in the trees. Eros hands Thanatos the ear trumpet. He listens. They look at each other and then out towards the forest. One by one, pairs of glowing eyes become visible from the trees and settle on the diners, reflecting the light from the candles. Eros sets down his knife and fork, leans back in his chair, and turns to Thanatos.

How's your head?

Better, Thanatos says.

Has the bleeding stopped?

Eros touches his ear lightly. He spits into a handkerchief and wipes dried blood from Thanatos's jaw.

Yes, it's stopped. What do you think they want from us?

Thanatos scans the edge of the forest. Shadowy bodies with shining eyes now form a complete circle around them.

Perhaps we're dessert, he answers.

Always seeing the bright side, Eros says.

Thanatos shrugs. The forest is full of hungry animals.

Eros stands and extends his hand. Well, let's at least provide the after-dinner entertainment.

Thanatos takes his hand. Eros draws him in. They begin to dance. The stereopticon shows images of a crimson bed piled high with pillows and a thick eiderdown coverlet. The sky above the clearing is black and pricked with stars. The circle of eyes edges a little closer. Eros and Thanatos hold each other and sway in time to the music.

Tangled in trees
in trees
in trees

THE WOLF, PART II

The black wool hood frames her face. Her hair sticks to her damp forehead. She hears the sound of breaking glass behind her, followed by a rustling in the trees.

She can't see his shadow, but she can feel it. She stands still and listens. A soft, insistent breathing. Is it his breath or hers? She isn't sure.

She may have dreamt this. She may already know the smell of him, the way his tongue travels so slowly over his teeth. Her heart beats a little faster.

LITTLE GHOST BIRD

Hey, little ghost bird
sitting on a branch.
When the sun goes down
you'll do your little dance.
You'll puff out your chest
and fluff up your wings,
while the moon rises slowly
and whispers secret things.

You can group or ungroup
the shards as you wish

THE WOUNDED FOX

Dusk. Darkness creeps inside all the pockets. The red fox rests beside a pink, trumpeted flower. It has injured its leg. There is glitter stuck in the wound. It catches the light.

The fox contracts its paw and slides it into the foxglove. Such a perfect fit. *Digitalis*. The fox could wear this flower glove to a dinner party and it would be a perfect thing.

If the fox were able to speak, you might ask, What are you doing, little fox?

With a sideways glance and a flick of its tail, the fox might answer, I am in the thicket, now and always. I am the jewel in the obscurity.

Your eyes would travel to its leg. Your wound—it's beautiful. Can I clean it?

The fox might shake its head. No. It heals as it shines.

With that, the fox turns and disappears into the darkness, leaving the foxglove and a trail of glitter on the path at your feet.

SANATORIUM

The light in the clearing is blue. Blue like her dress. The one with the white cross painted on it. He wears a charcoal suit. His black bird head glistens as he cocks it, looks first with one eye, then the other.

Earlier, he painted the white cross on the dress before she put it on. He hadn't been wearing anything except for a pair of thin black socks. The tip of his penis had touched the dress as he moved the brush. Two quick strokes. Down. Across. No drips. Clean and white.

The full moon hangs above them, above the trees. Here, under the leaves in the quiet of the night, dew settles into their clothes, the fine feathers of their heads, and the ferns of the forest floor.

I'm getting wet, she says.

He nods and removes his suit jacket, his tie, his shirt. The indigo plumage of his back catches the light. She coughs and a thin film of blood appears on her tongue. He places his coat across her shoulders and puts his mouth near the opening to her ear.

Say you'll always be mine in the wood.

I'll always be yours in the wood, she tells him, closing her papery eyelids.

THE FLÂNEURS' ARCADE

THE GRAND TOUR

You pack your bag with autumn in mind, autumn leading into winter. Layers.

You bring books to read on the train. You bring pens, pencils, a paintbox, brushes, a camera, blank notebooks, sketchpads, watercolour paper. Tools for documentation.

You leave home with one case and return home with three. A case for each month. You could bring back twice as much. You have to be selective.

People say it's about the journey, not the destination. Dialectical thinking has its limitations.

There is the smell of coffee. The sound of footsteps on cobblestones. The swish of rain and the sweep of leaves. The streets feel familiar and unfamiliar at the same time. You could keep walking forever. Taking photos. Collecting moments, impressions. Art and architecture of such depth and quality you want to weep. How is there so much intricate tile work? How long did it take to make such beauty? How much dedication and focus and care?

Sleeping past dawn feels wasteful. You prefer to be alert to the world. So much to see, smell, taste, record. You collect the scraps of ephemera that float endlessly through each day and press them between the pages of your notebooks. You stretch the days out like bread dough and watch them rise.

Same moon. Different birds. How is it that libraries are so beautiful? The square at night. Narrow streets behind the cathedral. Books in different languages. You get lost. You find your way. You remove your gloves and place something new in your case. You carefully build your collection.

GOLDEN TOWN

You walk through the city of a hundred towers.
A labyrinth of narrow streets spiders out around you.
Above you, on the hill in their crown chamber,
the royal jewels lie behind an iron door with seven locks.
The glass beads rest in your pocket.
The river flows beside you under the dark stone bridge.
The buildings are the colour of cake icing.
Creamy pink. Pale turquoise. French vanilla.
You want to run your tongue along them.
You run your fingers over the beads in your pocket instead.
Smooth and cool.
Blue and round.
The buildings hold space.
You float in the centre of their dream.

Think of it as an arcade
with light pouring from above

THE ANIMAL SOIREE

Mrs. Rabbit and Mr. Bull are running late, but are unflustered. She with her parasol, ruffled dress, collar, brooch, and shawl. He with his vest, striped dinner jacket, and silk cravat. Their arms are linked and they look devotedly at one another. A little rumpled, but certainly presentable.

Philomena Ruffle Bird and Trixie Cat Hat are on their way dressed in high collars, pompoms, and long gloves. Philomena's head feathers are particularly arresting and her violet fan is expanded to its full width, hiding the excitement fluttering in her corset. Bracelets over gloves, a small satchel clipped at the waist, Trixie has one hand on her hip, an answer ready for anyone who asks. Absolutely, we have escorts; they went on ahead.

Perhaps these three gentlemen in their military finery? From his carved chair at the head of the table, Sir Antelope has just popped the cork on the champagne. His tongue slavers as his comrades-in-arms, Sirs Lion and Tiger, look on. Crystal flutes at the ready.

At the next table, Ferdinand Fox, an accountant by trade, is sensible in his black tie, pinstripes, and spectacles. He has the attention of a demurely dressed but emotionally intense Ms. Kitty, who strains forward in her seat, hanging off his well-enunciated words. Although he is drinking a weak blackcurrant liqueur and appears quite lucid, she is flushed from her tumbler of brandy and her eyes have an unusual glow. Beside them, a plate of biscuits and a jar of preserves remain, as yet, untouched. How can an eligible cat think about food at a time like this? This could be it. He could be the one to organize all her ledgers.

A LETTER FROM THE CAPITAL

My darling,

Today I bought you something. I had crossed the bridge and was on Vítězná on my way towards Petřín when I noticed an antique shop on my right. A dusty statue of the infant Jesus at the back of the window caught my eye, so I went in.

The place teemed with nostalgic relics and was surprisingly organized for being full from floor to ceiling. My eyes immediately flooded with detail and I felt the whispers of thousands of stories pushing up against me.

When I asked the shopkeeper, he brought the statue out of the window and placed it in my hand. I knew immediately that I needed to buy it for you.

The infant is carved out of wood and the surface is painted with coloured wax. It is very fragile. When the shopkeeper found the statue, it had been abandoned in a pile of debris and its hands had been severed. The shopkeeper reattached the hands and, as he did, he received this message:

> *Have mercy on me and I will have mercy on you.*
> *Give me my hands and I will give you peace. The*
> *more you honour me, the more I will bless you.*

The infant's crown is held in place by a gold wire directly above his head, like a halo. He wears a red robe with white trim, but you could dress him in different-coloured robes if you liked—for example, rose to communicate subdued joy or green for life and hope. We could make these tiny clothes together when I return home.

I think of you always and count the days until we will be together again. Until then, your little prince sleeps in his box beside my bed and we dream of you.

From your treasure seeker, with all my love.
X

All of it is for you

THE TRUE SWEETHEART

There are coffee grounds on the snow beside a spattering of fresh blood. We walk by in our finery. I am wearing a dress with a flared mink skirt the colour of butterscotch. Your pompadour makes you exactly two inches taller than me.

People look at us as we pass. We shelter under a black umbrella; you hold the wooden handle and I have my arm through yours. We wear our wedding bands on opposite hands.

I loved you from the start and you were a slow burn. Then, after our suns met, they overlapped and shone in every weather. It is the overlap that people see when we walk by. You are coffee and I am blood and our arms are linked in some exotic combination of life and aromatics that electrifies the wet falling snow.

This is a very good day, we said in unison that morning. This will be the happiest day ever.

The snow falls all around us, our suns shine, and the fine wool of your jacket and the soft animal of my skirt dance. I think of a poem by D. H. Lawrence about being a drowsy cat at peace in the house of life, and you think about engine pistons and how built things fit perfectly together, and the snow turns to money and the ground piles up with it and we wade through the currency on our way to the party.

CARNIVALIA

THE ONEIROSCOPIST

You've been kept awake by vivid dreams.
Your friends give advice.
Go to the carnival, they say.
Lose yourself in the lights and the din.
Follow the sound of the theremin.
Visit the tent on the edge of the midway.
Listen to what the funny little man tells you.
He's the best dream interpreter this side of the river.
His words are simple and direct:
Things are not as you have been taught.
What you thought was blood was a metaphor for vital energy.
What you thought was scary was simply important.
What felt haunting only wanted you to be present.
Your instincts have brought you here.
Nothing is broken that cannot be repaired.
Remember who you are.

Think of it as a world
without end

THE BRIGHTNESS

The boy lives at the edge of town near the forest. Just before the forest is the mall. Beside the mall is a parking lot. The forest begins where the parking lot stops.

A carnival has come to town for a week. It is set up in the parking lot. The boy likes going after it has shut down for the night. He stands in the parking lot and gazes at the dark machines. The Spider. The Flying Teacups. Chair-O-Planes. The Scrambler. Their combinations of plastics and metals and nostalgia make him feel happy.

On the last night, he brings a girl to the carnival before it closes. Leaves are falling. Half the moon is orange. There is a bite in the air. The girl looks up at the sky.

The moon seems really three-dimensional tonight, she says.

He follows her gaze.

I have a bunch of glow-in-the-dark skeletons in a dish at my house, she tells him. Sometimes when I forget they're there, I turn out the light and it momentarily throws me.

He takes her hand and they walk towards the trees. Her voice is urgent against the night.

I don't want to live without the sparklers, the brightness. Without that feeling of lying flat on the ground, pressed down with barely any blood or breathing and barely even any bones. What good is living without that? Only TV and TV and TV.

I know, he whispers against her hair, his eyes closed. Let's go on a ride.

They walk together into the trees and he sings her a Christmas song while the music from the carnival plays in the background.

THE TAP DANCER

I'm falling through the sky with my hair streaming out.
I'm trying to remember who I am.

I have hazy memories of what it was like.
There was a studio with clamps, armatures, an exhaust fan.
Late into the night, I would scribble in bed
a notebook full of sketches open on my legs.

What happened?
How did I end up here, part of the sideshow,
suspended above the midway listening to the street organ
while commerce carries on merrily below me?

I used to be a creator.
Now my legs are loose and elastic,
as if they belong to someone else.
Miles away, my black shoes lever their way through the dance.
Toe tap, shuffle, flap, and swing.
I imagine the sound they'd make if I were on solid ground.
Bitty bing bitty bitty bing bang.
What good is an airborne tap dancer?
I am the lost inventor.

THE AMPUTEE

There was a problem with my leg. Some sort of aberration under the skin of my calf. I went to the doctor when I couldn't zip up my boots anymore.

This has to come out, she said, her lip a tight, thin line. Now the thing floats in a glass jar in my bedroom. It looks a bit like a sprouted potato. I keep it to remind me of what goes on beneath the surface.

I like my leg better since the operation. It stops above the knee. My prosthesis is custom-designed with smooth brass hinges at the joints. The knee is particularly handsome when viewed from behind. At night, it rests on an antique chair beside my bed. I close my eyes and rub the spot where my leg ends until I fall asleep. Sometimes, my lover likes to take the nub in his mouth and baptize it with his tongue. When he does, I remember the feeling of running.

THE ANCHORESS

By the time she was seven years old, she had received all five wounds of Christ. This was an embarrassment so she always wore shoes and gloves to school. Childhood and adolescence were difficult. Music saved her soul.

She married young. Her husband tried to make her wear a chastity belt, so she turned him from a wolf into a lamb. Now she is single and wears a horsehair girdle and a bracelet, gifted from the angels, hung with jingling stars.

She lives in a small trailer. Each day, an attendant straps her into a corset until her breath comes short and fast. She listens to music through her headphones while he feeds her sips of water.

People come to visit her little window. They help themselves to the stack of holy cards with her image from a wooden shelf beside the door. They whisper among themselves while she coruscates and issues forth.

Life is short! Accept your challenges as gifts! Everything has happened to me! I've been burned alive and am still whole. My eyes have lain on a silver platter and have grown back in my head. All things are possible! Listen to jazz for relaxation, classical for elevation!

When she is finished, she flies up from her chair and hovers near the ceiling while her attendant draws a red velvet curtain across the window. This is a sign for the visitors to leave, and they do.

In which we consider
hybrids of various types

THREE AUTOMATONS

The Levitator and His Bride

I stand, wearing a suit and tie, shiny black shoes, and red nail polish. I am a man. Beside me, my bride lies on a wooden platform wearing a lacy dress and white fishnet stockings, her blond hair in curls. We have worn these outfits for decades. We are always and forever fancy.

When I raise my hand slowly above her, my bride's body lifts up off the platform and hangs suspended in the air. I pass a large hoop back and forth around her length to show that she is floating. Then I lower my hand and her body gently returns to gravity.

This is what we do, she and I, over and over again. Always and forever fancy together in our ritual of lightness and weight.

The Head Remover

I am dressed in the style of my day. The yellowed lace of my collar contrasts pleasingly with my blue eyes. I stand onstage and a curtain comes down in front of my head. When the curtain lifts, my head has disappeared from my shoulders and reappeared inside a box I hold in my outstretched hand. I often feel a ripple of delight run through the audience, even though they know the trick.

The Young Minimalist

I used to have clothes, but they obscured my mechanics. Now you can see all of me: my wood-and-metal body, my ceramic arms, my legs attached with wire, my porcelain head. I shake my rattle all day long. Certain types of people can't take their eyes off me. Small children. Expectant mothers. Those fascinated by underpinnings.

THE DOLLS

We have porcelain heads with pink mouths
and realistic eyes that blink.
We are powered by keys
and spring-loaded windup mechanisms.
When the keys are released
the springs unwind to produce energy.
This makes us do interesting things
like cry and speak and move
parts of our bodies in unison.
We don't have a lot of words but you'll understand.
We operate as a team.
Wind us up and watch us go.

THE ROSE LADY

I had worked at the university for thirty years. That was the exact tenure of my hypnotism. Like all hypnotics, I didn't realize I'd been hypnotized until I became unhypnotized. One day, out of the blue, I woke up with a start and things were different. I blinked and surveyed my surroundings. It was like I was seeing the world for the first time. It was like I had just been born.

I grew roses for eyes. My eyes still worked perfectly, but when I blinked, the petals moved and there was the slight, delicate aroma. Somehow, this wasn't a shock to me. One thing I've learned is that everything has an antecedent. In the past, I would have spent a lot of time thinking about that, perhaps writing a paper about it. Not anymore. I left my job in academia and took my mind for a walk.

Now I'm a sensualist, not an intellectual. My job is to dehypnotize. People come into my tent carrying bits of nature. A pine cone, a special flower, an iridescent blue feather found in the park. I ruffle my rose petals to scent the air and use my inside eyes and ears to deliver the message. I'm a nature reader. A translator for the modern age. Most of my visitors are city dwellers who feel disconnected in the sea of technology designed to connect them. They call me the Rose Lady. *Close your eyes and inhale.*

The cracks in
between where all
the glitter falls

THE PRODIGY

He has an enormous head,
with exceptionally long eyelashes
and almost translucent skin traced with blue veins.
His bed is covered with books and mechanical toys
from another century
and his bedside is lined with glass medicine bottles.
During the day, he rests his head on a satin pillow
and dictates his thoughts into a small recording machine.
He takes breaks to sip water through a glass straw
and arrange his toys using a special mahogany stick.
Some say the large-headed boy is a forgotten prince,
abandoned due to his disfigurement.
Admission is fifteen cents for fifteen minutes.
His room is always well-attended,
particularly by children.

THE CAT MAN

The Cat Man is left-handed. He keeps several cats as pets and wears a silver ring in the shape of a cat. He has a habit of twirling the ring around and around his finger. His skin is rough and red. Cigarette smoke circles his head as he waits patiently for the tattooed woman to knock on his door.

There are evenings when he can't see her because she is getting more work done.

He'd have a fit if he knew, she had whispered. He's not the understanding type.

The Cat Man reached over and tucked her hair behind her ear.

Don't worry. We're just friends. How can he object?

Sometimes when she visits he can't touch her. Her skin is raw and needs to heal. The Cat Man clears his soft bed of cats and she lies down. He brings her hot coffee with brandy and pulls his chair up beside her. He reads aloud from his magazine while she rests. The indigo eye on her right bicep is always open, watching the Cat Man as he reads. The Tower of Babel on her forearm is forever falling. On her thigh, a brilliant cerulean Virgin Mary flexes when she shifts her leg. And on her chest, the newest addition is a wall of thorny roses glistening with traces of blood. The wall holds the skeletons of princes, trapped on their quest to find Sleeping Beauty, unable to pass through the thick hedge of flowers to the enchanted castle beyond.

While he reads, the Cat Man pauses often to watch her skin as she shifts on the bed. So many roses in so many colours. Burnt orange, yellow, pink, white. The pyramids, the entire lunar cycle, stretched across her abdomen, more memento mori skulls than he has been able to count, some as tiny as ladybugs, some strung together like beads around her wrists. He can't get enough. When it is late, she pulls on a gauzy cape that floats over her coloured skin and goes out into the night.

There is no question, her husband is good at his job.

THE VISIONARY

You pull aside the blue velvet curtain in the caravan behind the Ferris wheel, and this is what the visionary with glass eyes tells you:

I may be blind, but I can see that what you thought you'd lost is coming back to you across the stars, funnelling down through your dreams, straight into the place where you have felt missing and empty and untethered, without words.

This is it. Your pink rabbit ears, your lucky bell, your real home. No more fire in street lamps. No more burnt steak in passageways. No more melancholy robins' songs. These are cartoon days! Times of animation and cute monster faces. Like everyone else, you were fooled into thinking binaries were mutually exclusive. You didn't realize they were all crammed together in the same room. What a farce! What a ride! What a long, lean joke! Who told you it was serious? The courtyard has been full of liars for years.

No bother. Enough drudgery! Come unbound and fill the air with the gossamer of now! No need to live in two separate rooms, not quite here, not quite there. Your ghost heads are positioned at the portal. Your rings glitter in the light of the moon. A small bat of shame hangs wrinkled from your elbow. If you twirl, it will fly off and the trees will release their sap into your eyes and you'll see clearly. There's no fight here. Don't give another thought to propriety. The birds are lifting their wings!

NATURALIA

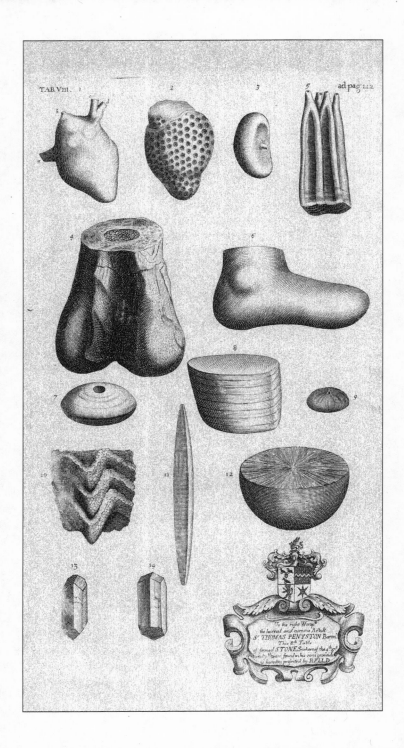

TAB. VIII.

ad pag. 112

RENAISSANCE MAN

When he can't sleep at night he often wanders into the mirabilia room. Standing in front of the cabinet, he jingles keys and slides open drawers. He allows his eyes and his mind to drift over objects, recalling the conditions of their acquisition. Particular smells, the quality of the air or light. His criteria are general, yet specific to his tastes: the wondrously fine, old, small, or delightfully unique.

His fingers glide across familiar surfaces. A ruby-encrusted music box containing a full set of crocodile teeth. A tiny upright skeleton of the genus *Felis*. Crystallized mineral specimens the colour of the night sky. A pale, spiralling unicorn horn from the sea. Five blue eggs in a nest beneath a bell jar. Three cabinet boxes of rare corals (*Korallenkabinett*), minus the elbow-shaped piece he had made into a protective amulet for his wife. A Venetian mask made of peacock feathers. The book of handwritten blessings his grandmother gave him when he was a child. A shadow box containing sixty-five varieties of iridescent beetle suspended on silver pins. A gold velvet bag containing Roman coins.

Sometimes in the morning his wife finds him curled up asleep on the carpet, wearing a gentle smile. She sits in a chair beside him, steaming cup of coffee in hand, and watches his eyelids flicker, until he stirs and the light comes back into his face. Through the window, she hears the morning sounds of boats and voices along the canal.

My darling, she says. You were dreaming. It's another miraculous day.

RABBIT FOOT CHARM

You didn't kill it.
You have no idea who killed it.
Perhaps it died of natural causes.
You like to stroke the foot when it's in your pocket.
You like the way the claws feel, partially covered by fur.
Perhaps its other feet are in other people's pockets.
Perhaps the rest of its fur sits softly
against the neck of a young girl in Finland.
Perhaps its flesh was cooked in a savoury stew
on a winter's evening, becoming part
of the muscle and bone and breath of the diners.
Perhaps every part of the rabbit's body
has been used and enjoyed.
Perhaps the rabbit is everlasting.
Your luck has never been better.

LIQUID SPECIMEN

My body is preserved in a jar of saline solution.
I can see you looking at me through the milky glass.
My soul is translucent.
I am a snake.
You used to be afraid of me, but now you're not.
I shed my skin more than once.
Milky, translucent skin.
It's what snakes do.
I'm floating above my body and so are you.
I see us looking at me.
I see you without your skin.
We're fresh and new together.

The object becomes
expansive

THE HEAD AND THE HAND

The fox has shiny black eyes and tawny fur. Its mouth is slightly smiling. A single hand protrudes from between its teeth. A doll's hand. Skin the colour of caramel.

The smiling fox wears a small gold crown between its ears. Perhaps this is why it smiles. Or perhaps it's because of the hand in its jaws. The fox doesn't have a body. The fox is only a head, stuffed and mounted, hanging on a wall. The fox's body is somewhere else entirely.

Perhaps the headless fox and the handless doll ran off together. The doll rides on the back of the fox as it carries her swiftly through the dark underbrush of the forest. The doll holds up her only hand to feel the cool breeze as they fly through the night. The fox relies on the doll's eyes and ears to guide them. She presses into his ribs with her thighs to direct their progress. A little to the right. Sharp turn to the left.

They travel by night and sleep by day in hollow tree trunks and under rocky ledges. They are the noise you hear through the shadows in the trees. They are the tracks in the mud. The fox and the doll will not stop until they have found what they have lost.

THE BLUE BEADS

Your shoes tapped the cobblestones as you crossed the street to gaze in the window. A little bell on the door rang as you entered. Picked things up. Set them down. A well-used deck of tarot cards. Musty books. Single china cups and saucers from someone's cabinet of favourites. You spotted a necklace made of blue glass beads. Blue like the sky. Blue, with a chalky feel in your hands. You bought the beads for five crowns. The man behind the desk slipped them in a clear plastic bag.

Back in your rooms, you realize that the necklace is filthy. You wash it in the bathroom sink with warm, soapy water. The silt of other people's lives, hands, and drawers turns the water brown. The glass comes to life. You lay the beads out on a towel to dry and they glow like translucent robins' eggs.

Later, when you dress for dinner, the beads make a pleasing sound in your hands. You wrap them around your wrist six times and wear them as a bracelet. It doesn't take long to discover their magic. The colour is almost electric. High up on the hill in the distance, the castle exerts its influence.

All of its facets turning

THE DISAPPEARING BIRD

Sometime in the dark season leading up to Christmas, a golden bird appears, fastened to a branch of the monkey puzzle tree. It is small and metallic, with a feathery tail.

Each day on my walk through the neighbourhood, I pass the tree with the bird and feel a thrill of delight that it's there among the branches. Visible but secret. How did it get there? Why? Is it possible it is just for me?

Weeks go by. There is rain, wind, snow. The bird weathers the storms and the days begin to lengthen. I revel in the sun and blossoming fruit trees and forget to look at the bird. Sometime in late spring, I realize it is no longer there. I grow sad and wish for the bird's return until, one night, I have a dream.

In the dream, my heart becomes the golden bird. It beats with the rhythm of wings and is brighter and more beautiful than ever before. My body becomes a tree, holding and enfolding the bird in its green branches. I know the bird is never going to leave me. My sadness disappears.

BABY

I haven't slept in years. I've forgotten what it's like. My arms and legs are painted white and I sit on the mantel beside the photos and the lamps. I am old and made of wood and linen and I have a chipped ceramic head.

I am a baby and I want you. I need you. I want you to come into this room and pay attention to me and hold me and stick something warm and soft in my mouth. I want the sound of your voice, even if I don't understand your words. I want the promise of your return.

I want you to carry me. I want to move around from one place to another in your arms. I want to smell you. I want to recognize your smell. I want you to feed me. I want you to rock me so I can finally drift off. I want to fall asleep knowing you'll never leave.

THE HAIRY ROOT

I am out walking to clarify my thoughts.
I find a sparkly thing on the sidewalk.
I take the thing and put it down
beside a tree in the park.
The thing is a glass eye.
I sit down under the tree.
I need the world to go quiet for a minute.
The glass eye becomes a fox and it says,
Here, take this, and hands me a Siberian ginseng root.
Take it home and use it to make a strong tea.
I nod and put the root in the breast pocket of my coat.
It is a little hairy
in the way that root vegetables sometimes are.
I think about teacups, and then
I hear a slight whizzing sound and realize
my grandmother is flying around
in the air above my head.
She sometimes does that during important moments.

Note the colour

SBC

The Squirrels' Boxing Club
is full of tiny, silky dukes
concealing claws good for all sorts.

Its members are united in their love
of a good-natured tussle between friends,
and the fight against germs,
rabies, and other destructive microbes;
one hundred percent committed to rodent hygiene.

Raising a glass together in the lounge after the main event,
and munching on nuts, they rub their knuckles
and frisk their tails,
talking of the merits of frequent paw washing
and caring not a fig for misguided public opinion
on the topic of vermin and other misnomers.

These nuts taste dusty, says a lovely grey to a weathered red.
They need a good rinse, Red agrees.
And a quick dry, to avoid mildew.
Just so, old man. Just so.
Tussle and rinse.
Dry and munch.

MECHANISM

The curator opens the glass case and winds the clock
with a golden key.
An owl in a cage with black eyes swivels its head
and taps its claws against a gilded perch.
Small bells ring in the cage.
A red fox crouches under metallic branches.
A rooster lifts its head and crows four times.
A squirrel holds a silver nut forever.
In the centre of the case, a peacock spreads its tail feathers
and spins in a circle, displaying its plumage.
I am beautiful, I am beautiful, I am beautiful, it says.
Hear the hours.

Note the glisten of the wing

THE WINTER PALACE

THE LITTLE MONKEY

Like all eccentric princesses, you once had a pet monkey.
You called him Sweet Knees.

He was a gift from your father, who brought him back
from one of his adventures in faraway lands.

Sweet Knees runs away from the castle during a holiday party
as guests were coming and going through the palace doors.

Because you trust in the rightness of things,
you don't grieve his departure for long,
but you do sing a farewell song in your bedroom
by the light of the moon on the night he disappears.

Hey little monkey
dancing on the snow
with a sparkle
and a shine
and a heigh-ho-ho.

THE GIRL WHO LEFT
THE PAST BEHIND

Her world was white creamy vanilla icing,
silk dresses, porcelain dolls.
Her world was parties, passageways, fireplaces,
wings beating against golden bars.

In her room, a tattered scrapbook lies open on the desk.
Those days are over. It's time to move on.

A sudden gust of wind billows the lace curtain out,
ghosting the night.
She is packed.
The birdcage is empty.

Her hand rests on the doorknob one last time.
Her eyes flutter open and closed.
She can feel the future with all its colours.

CATHEDRAL

Snow falls through an opening in the trees. It covers the ground and clings to tree trunks and branches. It keeps falling, day and night. The snow turns the woods soft and quiet. You stand in the clearing, breathing in and out, letting the tiny crystals cover you. Nothing is quieter than this elemental architecture, this internal palace of the mind.

THE PRINCESS ROOM

She walks through the neighbourhood. Her dirty-white coat is edged with fur. Her hat, a matching edifice on her head. Her hair, long and brown and loose. Her skin, waxy and white. Her legs, conspicuously bare under her short skirt. Her boots, white.

She has been reading the Russians. Tolstoy. *Anna Kare-nina*. Men in tall fur hats are stacked by her bedside table like a tower of ice. She's thinking of the Church of the Transfiguration and its twenty-two wooden domes, empty during the winter months. She's thinking of white swans in white snow. She doesn't care about fitting in. She is the star of her own Nordic mythology.

At the top of her house in the city there is a circular room with blue walls and a blue ceiling. At night, when it is lit up, the room becomes a sphere full of sky visible to the street below. If a grown man were to stand beneath her window, she might write him a message and tie it to the foot of a bird: *Not a Rapunzel story*. Whose scalp can take that kind of strain?

Resting in a cupboard on a wooden stand is a hinged enamel egg that opens to reveal a tiny gold castle. Keep this close, her mother had said, handing her the heirloom years ago. Use your imagination. Wear your crown on the inside. Always remember this majestic hollow.

The home inside
the home
inside the home

THE SNOW QUEEN

You have been journeying for eons.
Speeding across the snow in your sledge,
through holly and ivy.
The swoosh of the runners scraping away
seconds, minutes, years.
Gliding over the glittering crust,
and under trees with icy branches that would sound
like chimes if you gathered them up in your arms
all at once.

Certain distractions spring up and then
fall back into obscurity.
The dark trees around you shrug off
their loads in your path,
the thud of snow a temporary blockage, that's all.
Your sledge shows you it can levitate,
ride the obstruction like a wave.
You never dreamed it could be so easy.

You fly through the tops of trees,
eating the stars with your eyes,
the snow below reflecting all that light.
As if there had never been any reason for unhappiness.
As if all you had to do was believe in what you wanted
and it would happen.

You dream that diamonds appear in heaps
beside your pillow.
You offer your bag of treats to the little girl
who nods by the fire and she is the one
who stays with you for all of your life.
Is the castle off in the distance,
or is it just behind your sternum?

The forest is alive with twinkling lights.
Red. Yellow. Blue. Green. Gold.
Birds fluff their feathers in the crooks of trees.
The fox on the seat next to you nestles
its nose inside the perfect circle of its tail.
The crystalline world shines below and above.

The joy of
the secret

PATIENCE

I am in the castle.
It is snowing outside.
In my window, a candle burns against the night.
The fox is in the wardrobe cleaning its whiskers.
You are on your way to me.
The wallpaper is alive and flowers grow up the walls.
I breathe in their smell and count the hours.

HOW TO BECOME A PRINCE

Listen! The princess has been in the gold castle at the top of the glass mountain for seven years. Every suitor who tries to reach her falls to his death below. The mountain is littered with the decaying corpses of men and horses.

Young man, fasten yourself firmly to the glass! Sleep sweetly, deeply for a time, waking only to seize the feet of the huge eagle. Allow the bird to lift you high in the icy air, to circle around the castle's tower. The moon offers a dim lamp to the glittering palace below.

Hang on! Be patient and wait for the bird to set you down. The princess has trained it well. This is an exercise in cooperation. Be a hero and your world will fill up with golden apples in all seasons.

The museum was once
a private mansion

CATHERINE, EMPRESS
OF ALL THE RUSSIAS

My boots are noiseless in the long marble corridor.
I pass silk-covered walls and row
upon row of gold-framed paintings.
Sculpture, porcelain, engraved gems,
cameos, musical clocks, inlaid cabinets.
I command this vast collection of antiquities and beyond.

The sleigh waits outside the main palace entrance.
Slight gasp, the air a brace to my lungs.
Two black horses, bells jingling as they shake their heads.
Whinnies.

Snow swirls down from the grey sky. White upon grey.
The sun a pale orb, forever away from now.
I nestle under layers. Fur. Upon wool. Upon fur.

My buried necklaces clink like distant icicles.
A snap of reins and click of the driver's tongue.
A slight jolt forward, then we're on our way.

Today I am the passenger, though I am always the driver.
Other days I'm in the saddle wearing a man's uniform.
Breaking the crust of snow. Breaking the day in half.
It is my job to be confident. It is my job to rule.

THE ARTISTS' COLLECTION

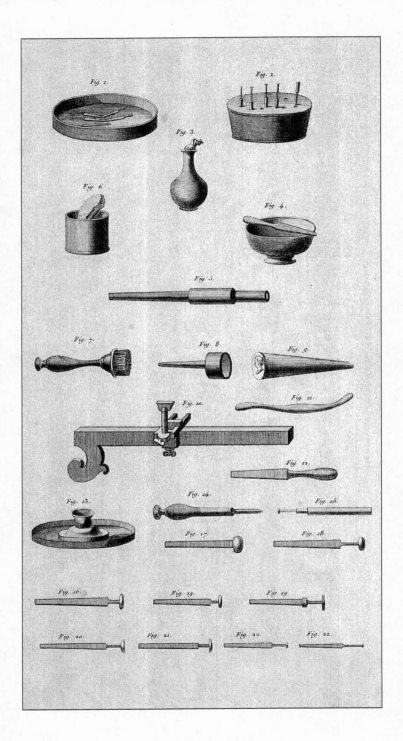

PORTRAITS

I wear my gold hoop earrings with the posts sticking out of the front of my earlobes. I'm always looking for a new way of doing things.

My father once made a figure out of an orange peel at the dinner table and told everyone that it was me. All it had between its legs was a couple of white, dangly orange-rind threads. Everyone laughed. When he did this, a voice inside me whispered, You'd better grow up!

I've been making things of my own ever since.

I helped with my parents' tapestry business when I was a girl; once, when the worker from the Gobelins factory couldn't come to help, I stepped in. This is how I learned to sew and draw.

When I'm awake during the night I use whatever scrap of paper is nearby. I write words, scribble, and jot. I burn holes. I take whatever comes. I trust my unconscious. There are always coloured pencils and pens and boxes of matches in the cupboard beside my bed. I am never without my supplies.

Is surrealism unfashionable? Is psychological inquiry embarrassing? I don't care. I don't pay attention to trends. I do exactly as I please. I draw things at all times of the day and night. I don't take notice of the time. If I'm awake and there's a piece of paper somewhere, I'm busy.

When I made my latex self-portrait, I was an adult. It started out flat and whitish and flexible, but it ended up much smaller, and eventually turned the colour of a lemon candy. The air crumpled it as it dried. It had a black smudge on one side that looked like a droopy eye, and the edge where it folded over itself got pressed together so that it looked like a pair of yellow lips. These lips, they were really stuck together.

I took the dried lemon face and sewed it with pink thread onto a pink piece of paper. It didn't take much to attach it. Just a few loops of thread to keep the face in place. Well, I hung that piece of paper on my wall and laughed. My father had been such a jackanapes. I showed him. I'm always showing him.

CHANDELIER

The poet writes like a demon through the afternoon and past dusk. Finally, he leaves his room and goes to hear a reading at the national library, with its many small windows. Inside his coat, he carries a sheaf of work kept uncrumpled by a stiff piece of cardboard.

After the reading, he cuts through the field beside the library. The air is thick with humidity. Some weather is blowing in. Out of the corner of his eye, the poet sees the long slash of colour that is the graffiti wall. He sees the bushes at the edge of the field and senses the blue fox in the underbrush. Its silken body glitters with jewels, hidden at the edge of the park.

When he reaches the top of the escarpment, it begins to rain. Wind moves the clouds around and small raindrops pebble the poet's back. He passes in front of a Victorian mansion and peers in through the leaded glass windows of the front door. He sees a lit chandelier. Its sparkling light reaches past the glass and the rain, straight into his eyes. He closes them and soaks up the grandeur.

Inside the house, a woman burns her hand while pulling a tray of cookies from the oven. Upstairs, a young man and woman lie bathed in candlelight. A wooden table is strewn with cake and broken teacups and spilled wine. In another room, under a bed, a girl takes apart a Russian doll and puts it back together, again and again. In the attic, a tall man with broad shoulders and a strong body applies white makeup to his face. Life is a house with countless floors and passageways. The poet knows this.

Soft rain washes the city. It creates reflections on the roads, brings up the smell of the ground, the trees, the small mosses that grow in concrete cracks. The poet feels no need to rush. The colours from the chandelier's crystals scintillate behind his eyes. Aquamarine, gold, cherry, emerald. He walks slowly and breathes in the night air. A voice in his head tells him: You're building a city. Each poem is a spire. The spires cluster together. Soon bells will ring. He smiles. Knowing that the blue fox is out there winking in the dark brings him happiness.

THE SISTERS STRANGE

The girls sit surrounded by candles in the alcove window of their garret. They make fantastical clothes with an old black Singer that sings and sings when it sews with its silver foot.

They play games on the big brass bed. Dress-up, make-believe, hats and wigs, and you be the mother and I'll be the father, you be the girl and I'll be the boy, let's all pretend we're boys for a change.

They have an old turntable and a pile of scratchy records. They sing along with *The Magic Flute* and Handel's *Messiah*, black stars sparkled with silver glitter drawn on their cheeks. Crochet hooks lie scattered across the wooden floor, along with balls of wool and wire and fabric scraps and pairs of scissors in the shapes of birds.

Over time, their creations have become less like clothing and more like sculptures. Dresses with secrets sewn into pockets and hems. Sweaters that reach the floor, organza trains that hang over the balcony and catch in the breeze. Animal and mineral shapes. Hard to get a coat over.

The sisters sit smoking pipes at all times of the day and night, tapping the bowls against the iron railings, sending small rains of tobacco swirling down. Their names are Priory, Tether, Jima, Link, and Stella. They have each other. They have the things they make. Their dollhouse world smells like beeswax and vanilla smoke and they want for nothing.

The secret to life is

DEMOLITION

They were tearing down the house. You came during the night to take photos. The fridge door was off its hinges. The kitchen cupboards had no doors. A single glass and a plate sat on the counter beside the sink. Someone had left a kettle on one of the lower shelves. The startling thing was the hole ripped in the kitchen wall. Because the house was on a hill, the view afforded by the hole was spectacular. Down past a black band of trees, the city rose up against the sky like a belt of diamonds. The lights from the buildings funnelled through alleyways straight into your chest. You thought you would burst. You left, forgetting to take a single photo. Now the house is gone and something new is being built in its place, and you'll never forget that shining moment.

THE GROUPIE

She spends her days and nights making watercolour pictures on thick white paper for rock stars to hang up in their buses and dressing rooms.

She doesn't want them to touch her and they never try. She just paints and paints, her hands spilling out colours. Sometimes she uses her best squirrel-hair brushes to trail glitter on their faces so they sparkle onstage.

You can't judge a book by its cover, she says, when she says anything.

And she just laughs when people call her jailbait and accuse her of sleeping with all those damn rock stars with their dreamy poet eyes and tattoos.

You don't know anything, she thinks, and mixes up the pink.

DR. MÜTTER'S 19TH-CENTURY DREAMING

I dream of medical reform.
I dream of beautiful monsters.
I dream of vials of green and white pills
good for living and dying.
I dream of prosthetics and movement.
I dream of anaesthesia and the sleep of transformation.
I dream of suspended animations
in glass jars with tidy labels.
I dream of connective tissue, of linkages,
of fissures and joinings.
I dream of twins and brains and skulls and recoveries.
I dream of an end to suffering.
I dream of learning and teaching
and showing and knowing.
I dream of becoming, of unbecoming,
of leaving and arriving.
I dream of a museum of singularities.
I dream that every body is perfect.

THE GROUNDSKEEPER

A fence separates Estrella's house from the rest of the park. At night, the lights from her windows cast golden pools out into the trees. The nocturnal animals rustle, scamper, shift from one downy foot to another on branches. Owls hoot. Foxes scream. Frogs croak. The ecosystem runs itself. Estrella tends the grounds, makes sure that park users don't feed the animals, keeps an eye on things. No cages here.

Lately, she has been taking a lot of photos. Old-school-style, on film. Of the animals, of the naked tree branches against the sky, of the sky at dusk and dawn, of her own weathered hands. While the animals make their noises during the night, she develops film in a makeshift dark-room she's set up in the laundry closet. Photos hang to dry above the sink. She's experimenting with sepia. Portrait of a rabbit, running. Portrait of trees haunted by winter. Portrait of a fox carcass under the blackberry bushes. A snow-white feather floating slowly from tree to ground. Sometimes when you live by yourself, you need a bit of company; you need to make something out of nothing to know you exist.

You can't abandon yourself

THE HERO'S JOURNEY

You're standing beside a security guard in an artist's installation designed to make you think about memory, identity, stories. Scratchy music plays on hidden speakers and there are books, record players, photos, old furniture. The security guard's ID badge says his name is Joseph Campbell. He walks through the gallery, tracing the same path around its perimeter, over and over. He walks across bubble wrap and pops it with his heels, like he's part of the installation. He seems to want to get your attention. Maybe he has a message just for you: You enter the forest at the darkest point, where there is no path. You're here to find your way. You're here to get hold of your myth! He repeats this with his shoes and the bubble wrap and his voice that echoes in your head without a single movement from his lips and you feel a wave of emotion break over you like glass.

THE SQUIRREL PAINTER

My name is Mr. Flesk. What I do is this: I go around the city and spray-paint squirrels in unlikely places. Mostly at the edges of things. Sometimes black ones, sometimes red. I have a stencil. I hang around outside the Squirrels' Boxing Club and take photos of the members as they come and go. You may be making your way through an underpass when you see one of my squirrels out of the corner of your eye, where the wall meets the sidewalk. Small and pristine. Perfectly represented. No mange on my squirrels. There aren't enough squirrels in cities these days. This is because there aren't enough trees. Or parks. A squirrel needs a habitat. A place to build a nest and sleep. Some nuts to gather. No trees, no nuts.

THE NIMBLE ROBOT

You dream that you build a robot entirely out of art supplies. Easel skeleton. Canvas stretcher bars and metal rulers for arms. Pencils and pens and paintbrushes of various sizes for fingers. Linseed oil to grease the joints. A raw linen smock with pockets for scissors and pastels, with their creamy textures and colours. The smell is fantastic.

As soon as you finish building it, the robot begins to move. Sketchbook pages fly. Paintings and drawings and objects begin to assemble in unique configurations. As in all dreams, it is as if you are the observer and the actor simultaneously.

You wake up with a profound feeling of satisfaction. You are what you do. It is the robot's job to make art every single day. There is no end to its streaming.

Your inner kingdom

THE DANCERS

The dancer makes her clothes out of rags, scraps, bits of this and that, here and there. Vintage, a scattering of sequins, a scrap of old lace, part of a sweater, a necklace made of star anise, with its exquisite shape and smell. On the street below her window, yellow taxis travel in lines and the snow melts when it hits the black pavement. She walks down the street wearing her one-of-a-kind outfits and nobody gives her a second glance. You have to do a lot in this city to be noticed.

There's the old building where she rehearses and performs, with its worn marble stairs and its bluish-green walls. There's the subway stop. There's the building where she lives. There are the postcards taped to the kitchen cupboards and the clothes draped over chair backs and the sewing machine and the vanity table and the stool and the lamp with the white glass shade she's had since she was a girl. There's the lack of tidiness and the many projects in various states of completion.

The dancer's uncle died when she was eighteen and left her an inheritance. She was always his favourite. After the funeral, she took part of the money and bought herself a condo in the sky, where she floated and did some math and dreamed of what to do next. According to her calculations, she was equipped to dance and sew and watch the stars orbiting over her head for longer than she would be on earth. So she counted her lucky stars and relaxed and made pot after pot of loose-leaf Earl Grey tea in the early mornings.

One of her friends died from a lack of food and another has decaying teeth from a lack of keeping food down, so the dancer is careful to eat. She makes clothes for her dancer friends and they perform together in shows, which handfuls of people attend, but it is art and the numbers don't matter.

No boy will ever love you as much as I do, her uncle told her when he was wasting away from a mysterious ailment. No boy will ever love you with a heart so pure.

So far, it was true. Once, in high school, she had made a jacket with moss sewn into it for a boy she liked, and when she gave it to him, he laughed.

What is this, a tree costume? he said, and left it sitting on the park bench in the rain.

The boys she knows now like the clothes she makes. They strut and preen and watch the sun glint off the shiny bits. They kiss the air around her head and tell her she's a fashion genius. They adore her leg warmers and corsets and the way the star anise smells when the heat gets in. They all dance together in the great city while the stars turn in their orbits light years away.

TWIN BROTHERS

The brothers are in an ancient city at night. Awake and dreaming in their workshop, their hands twitch with papier mâché, pale puppets with fragile faces. Their work table is scattered with scissors, bits of decaying dolls (babies with smashed noses, babies with the tops of their heads missing), screws, scraps of metal, pulleys, thread, a wooden comb.

Outside the studio window, a tram slides past the cathedral. Images flash like a film reel. Cyrillic advertising text. Stained glass windows. A giant head of the Virgin Mary. Obscure metal structures make clanking noises. Possibly the tram, possibly the scaffolding on the church, possibly the gears of the universe.

Inside, at the table, everything is in motion. Objects seem to move by themselves. Screws twist and turn amidst piles of sawdust. Dolls' eyes blink, spinning dreams of dandelions and grass and pretty dresses. One of the brothers thinks, I am the forest. One of the brothers thinks, I'm more alive now. Their identical hands are busy building.

THE DIORAMISTS

My true love and I built a diorama together before we met each other. If you've ever fallen in love, you'll know what I mean. It was as if he and I pressed our foreheads together and decided without words what our home would look like. Now the diorama is where we live our lives. Its backdrop is the world and it contains everything beautiful and magical and unexpectedly delightful that you could want from a partnership.

My shoes are part of our diorama. His black cat is part of our diorama. My morning toast is part of our diorama. At night, when it is dark outside the diorama, I am not afraid. The ocean laps against our shore, like amiable bathwater. The moon is the biggest and most stunning moon you can imagine. Every house I can see from our bedroom window when I'm lying in bed looks like some version of a castle. In the morning, when I wake up to the sounds of birds outside sounding like some sort of mythical Eden, I think, This is my life, my glorious life.

How unrealistic, you say. Well, not really. Anyone can build a diorama. It's not difficult to transform some cardboard with paint and wallpaper and lifelike greenery and other props. These are important skills any modern person should possess. What you make with your hands becomes real. Don't waste your breath telling me you're not creative. Dioramas are for everyone. Your body expands beyond itself. Your arms are wide enough to hold it all.

Carry it with you

FRANZ

He paces from side to side in the glass display case, grop-ing for the door. Small. Angular. Surrounded by notebooks. Wearing a black suit and making himself sick with black thoughts: *Hopelessness of the future. Dread of night. What-ever I touch crumbles to pieces.*

He doesn't see that the case has no top. When he dies, his heels twinkle together briefly before his soul lifts up and out through the opening. Finally free.

APPARITIONS

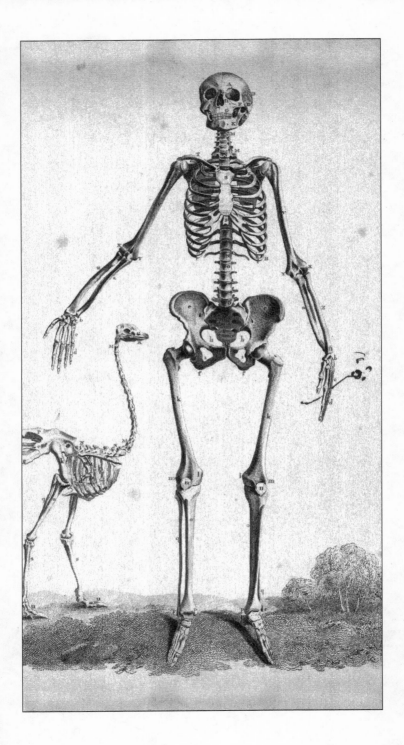

SPOOKY LITTLE THINGS

To banish spooky, echoing thoughts, it is best to dwell on merry thoughts. Take something that represents the spookiness and place it in the sun. Do whatever witchy thing you have to do to transform the spooky thing into a happy thing. Tap it with a stick. Sprinkle it with glitter. Sing it a song. Whatever it takes. Distract yourself. Once you've mastered this, the world belongs to you. Take it from us, the dearly not departed.

This is a holographic world

THE ARM

I live in a ruined castle on the edge of a tousled moor. At night, the wind whips around the edges of the turrets, loosening the ages-old stones and diminishing the architecture in tiny increments.

When I was a child, my parents died in a freak accident involving a swan, a runaway horse pulling a sled over fresh snow, and an icy incline towards the sea. I was raised by my aunt and uncle and an assortment of cousins of various ages, all the while assured that being an orphan brought with it a cachet of undeniable mystery and romance. And so I believed in the perfection of life from an early age.

I suppose, at one time, the castle had been quite grand, but in the true spirit of British eccentrics, my adopted parents had let it slide slowly into a well-loved tumble of old velvet draperies, chipped gold picture frames, and peeling wallpaper.

My favourite places were the attics, which were repositories for what were, to me, the most fascinating objects. Antique prams. Iron bed frames. Boxy suitcases peppered with destination stickers. Piles and piles of books.

One day, I found an old wooden box with a hinged lid. When I opened it up I saw a prosthetic arm made of wood and metal. It was etched with the name Lucinda Blythe in a curly black script. When I looked down at my two young arms, all of the fine blond hairs were standing on end. I quickly put the arm back in its box and closed the lid.

Now I spend my days carefully reading on my bedroom window seat, keeping watch over the world outside and having inside adventures. My name is Lucinda Blythe and I am thirteen years old.

SKELLIES

I remember because it was early October and the carnival was passing through town. We could hear the music from the midway and catch a whiff of popcorn on the air when the wind was blowing just so. The leaves were red and it was often rainy. Halloween was coming.

We'd had problems with our plumbing and a guy had come to lay down some new pipe in the backyard. He was out there digging when he found the skeletons. Two of them with the bones perfectly intact. Of course, there was a rigmarole and the police came to collect them, but not before my sister and I got a good look.

The coroner said that they had been two middle-aged women. Maybe they had lived in the house before we did. Maybe they had been sisters, like us. I wondered if someone buried them on purpose or if they died in the yard and were buried by time. Their bony faces looked like they were smiling, but maybe all skeletons look like that.

Not long after the discovery, I took my umbrella and went to the store to buy some undershirts and licorice and an alarm clock. They were selling Halloween candy and costumes. I saw skeletons there, too, some with plastic eyeballs, some without.

Now I sometimes find myself thinking about the backyard skeletons when I am alone in the house. This makes me feel a little uneasy, like maybe I should be afraid of them, even though they aren't there anymore and hadn't seemed scary at the time.

When my sister gets home, I tell her my worries. To make peace with the skeletons, she says, all I have to do is imagine sending them light beams from my own eyes into their eye sockets. She says that this will make everything friendly between me and the skeletons, that it will project good feelings straight into their skulls, and won't leave room for anything else. She's quite matter-of-fact when she tells me this, as if she were describing how to boil an egg.

THE CRYSTAL RING

Those were the early days of photography. The days when I still had him. The days of hat pins and watch fobs. Those were the days before he left me. The days of garden parties and the future. The days before I became the saddest woman in the world.

Then came the days of weeping veils and jet. I made a ring from his hair. A buckle, too. I fastened myself up tight with it and never stopped crying. I walked under a black parasol. I wrote my letters on black-edged paper. Wiped my eyes with black-embroidered handkerchiefs. Repeated his words to me: Love me forever. I grew my hair my whole life without ever cutting it again. It wrapped around my head like a tower.

Now, listen. He's gone and I'm gone but we're not far away. We float together. I'm giving you this crystal ring containing a coil of my hair. I had it made before I died. Carry it with you. Think of me. I'm in the air around you. Not lost, just gone before. Never forget we love you. There is no real separation.

Evolution is effortless
and effervescent
and never-ending

THE TOWER

The natural history museum is full of dead things and their ghosts. There is a central tower with sixteen glass windows in the ceiling. A low wooden railing curves up the staircase to the top floor. Soon after the building was completed, the tower began to sink into the earth. The architect saw this as a failure and threw himself from the roof. Sometimes when you visit, you see it wouldn't be difficult to quietly slip over the railing and fall to the lobby below.

At night, if you look up from the street, you can see the herbarium glowing on the top floor. If you were to sit on the bench beside the window, you would smell plants, the rows of bottles containing powders and pellets and dried bark. The room smells like life.

One floor down, an Arctic fox in a diorama is curled into a heat-conserving posture, with its white tail curled over its paws and nose. When environmental conditions become severe, forms of dormancy greatly reduce energy consumption by lowering the body temperature and reducing the heart rate. The sea mammals live one floor below the fox. Inside their flippers, seals and whales have bones that look just like the bones in human hands and fingers.

When the architect fell from the tower, it was dusk. His head led his body, as if he were launching from a diving board into a pool of turquoise water. He still hovers in the light.

THE GIRL WITHOUT A BODY

I ate a handful of poisonous berries and died. I floated up in my old-fashioned pinafore costume and dropped bits of lace upon the earth until my family looked out their windows and said, Look, it's snowing in July.

My body was still beside the bush where I had curled into a ball, holding my belly. My sister discovered me and ran inside to get my mother, who wiped her apple-nutmeg-butter-pastry fingers on her apron before running out and finding my mouth and fingers stained purple.

I rode with the siren and the white interior of the ambulance and my mother's face leaning in, but it was too late. I wanted to touch my mother's head and tell her not to cry.

I'm happy, and it was not hard or painful to go. A bug crawled across my cheek, a cardinal sang, a butterfly bobbed past and then I lifted up.

Now I am the pinafore ghost who hovers around the house of her family. A sweeter haunting there has never been. I cover the summer grass with drifts of snow that carry my messages:

Let us rejoice in the physical world.
Let us rejoice in the non-physical world.
Let us rejoice in living.
World without end.

If I keep dropping my lace, one day they will hear me and look up with smiles on their faces, and they will finally understand that there is no cause for sadness.

Always the forward momentum

TRANSPARENCIES

In a train station in Europe, there is the smell of coffee. We hover amidst the hubbub. A man writes in a notebook with a fountain pen. People kiss goodbye and hello. Someone wears a hat made of peacock feathers. Bells chime harmoniously over the loudspeakers to chart time.

We look at pastries in glass cases, remembering the taste of cream. For days after I fell from the tower, you wore nothing but a fur coat and the necklace I gave you on our fifth wedding anniversary. Sweet lamb. I tried to console you, but you were unreachable. Now we're together, disembodied lovers forever haunting beautiful spaces.

In a café, a woman steams her face over a cup of tea and closes her eyes. You know what she is thinking, as do I. We come in close and hold her. She straightens up a little and opens her eyes. A child cries once and then stops. A seated man plays a cello and the music rises up to fill the station's ceiling dome. Now there is the smell of baking bread. Now the bustle of footsteps and the voices of so many people. We draw near and feel through them. See through them.

A man sits cross-legged in a quiet corner of the station and meditates while everything moves around him. People run into each other's arms. Energy streams. It will always be this way.

SUBLIME MONSTERS

SALT

The brown-haired woman lies awkwardly on her side of the brass bed, beside the lobster. Her eyes are half-open in a lazy gaze and her hands are pressed together between her thighs. On the wood-panelled wall beside the bed is a long rectangular painting of an ocean scene. Whitecaps foam on the tops of dark waves.

The woman is here in a cottage near the sea where she lives with her husband. Her husband becomes a lobster at night and switches back to a human at eight in the morning. It's a quarter to eight. He's returned from his nocturnal beach wandering and is now waving his feelers and clicking his claws against the pillowcase while he sleeps. Every couple has its problems.

When the clock over the mantel strikes eight and his crustacean body unspools back into the body of a man, she looks over at him.

What were you dreaming of?

Was I clicking?

Yes.

Sorry. Did it wake you?

I was already awake.

Everything okay?

Yes. Just thinking.

About what?

Nothing. Well, about children, I guess.

We've talked about that. You know it would be too complicated.

Yes.

He takes her in his arms.

Can't you find a way to be happy, just the two of us?

Her eyes are closed. A tear slips out and runs down her temple. He licks it. She pulls away.

You and your salt water. I don't even like the ocean.

Now she's crying for real, her sobs shaking the bed. He holds her. She breathes in mouthfuls of his dulsy smell. After a while, she quiets down and lies still beside him.

What can I get you?

She sighs.

Tea. Lots of milk. Toast. Marmalade.

He stands up. His body is slim and bronzed. Perfectly proportioned. She watches him pull on his pants.

Beautiful, she murmurs under her breath.

He glances back. Did you say something?

She shakes her head and shows him her teeth.

Okay. Don't move. I won't be long.

His back disappears down the stairs. The woman burrows beneath the sheets and curls her body small and hard like a beetle. From her nest, she can hear the pulse of the ocean through the open window. The sheets are damp and gritty with sand. She breathes rhythmically, high in her chest. Soon her husband will bring the tray and they will eat. Then they will make love and she will not get pregnant because children shouldn't have a father who disappears every night and always smells of brine.

ARCADIA

It's Halloween. The five friends rendezvous in the parking lot beside the funeral home at eight o'clock. Daylight savings time is over. Squirrels are hidden away in the trees. Night comes early now. There's the pop-pop-pop of firecrackers. Jack-o'-lanterns flicker from porches and short ghosts float from house to house clutching bags of candy. Weasel Boy has brought his German shepherd. The rain has stopped. Blue fog drifts slowly behind dripping trees.

The pale one who smells like vodka and fermenting apples hops a stone fence and walks with his arms out. He bends down to pick up a spring-loaded needle that's lying in the grass.

Huh, he says.

The girl with the flame-red hair frowns. Gross. Put it down.

He shrugs and lets it drop.

They head towards the outbuilding above the beach. The air is salty and waves roll quietly in the dark. A long release of air signals the presence of killer whales nearby. The friends try to spot the pod, but the moon is hidden by clouds.

The wooden building looms suddenly through the cedars. Somewhere in the forest, a night bird whistles its echoing song and the notes spiral away and away, deep into the trees. The five friends climb the creaky stairs. The dog stands still and sniffs the air. Something burning. Pumpkin flesh. Woodsmoke. Apple Vodka takes out a pocket knife and jimmies the lock on the door.

Inside, the girl wearing black plastic glasses unzips her bag and hands a string of coloured lights to the girl with the jet-black eyes. They start tacking the lights to the wall.

Weasel Boy prepares his Bacchus costume. Leafy crown. Sarong. A few bottles of wine. Apple Vodka plugs in the stereo. Flame Red draws a black star on her cheekbone with eyeliner and starts laying out food on a table in the corner. Bread. Cheese. Potato chips. Pieces of dark chocolate. A plate of pink sliced meats.

Soon, Jet Black has a bottle of beer in one hand and a cigarette in the other. She has taken off her sweater and is swaying to the music. An old song by the Cars plays on the stereo. *Right here your hands are soft and creamy.* Flame Red is putting another hole in Jet Black's ear. She holds the alcohol-soaked cotton swab behind her friend's lobe and positions the needle above the skin.

Stand still. I can't do this if you're dancing around.

Jet Black takes a drag of her cigarette and closes her eyes. You can be bossy.

Plastic Glasses is lying on the floor reading a book with a flashlight and eating rolled-up deli meat. Apple Vodka sidles up next to her and starts creeping his cool hands across her fairy costume. She tries feeding him some meat to distract him. He turns his head and whispers in her ear.

Trick or treat. No food to eat. It's your belly that's truly sweet.

She rolls her eyes and pushes him away.

Weasel Boy sits in an orange armchair and drinks from a bottle of wine while Jet Black performs a burlesque. The moon emerges momentarily from behind the clouds and lights up a strand of red beads against Jet Black's collarbone. Her ear is bleeding a little. Weasel Boy smiles through wine-stained lips, a scattering of burgundy drops glowing darkly on his chest. Flame Red's eyes glint as she looks on.

There's a wind picking up. On the beach, the waves crash against the sand and bare rocks, while under the surface of the water, the killer whales let out their low, musical groans. Inside the wooden building, the friends turn up the music. Outside, its fur blown backwards, the dog digs up a skull from the forest floor.

We could call this
the Museum of Becoming

THE CYBORG CYCLOPS

Odysseus and his men came into my cave and ate my food, so I ate some of them. Then they lured me to sleep with strong wine and lanced my only eye with a hot, sharpened spear. Odysseus told me his name was Nobody, so my cries of Nobody has blinded me! Nobody has blinded me! went unheeded across the island where I lived.

It all worked out in the end. The fake eye is even better than the real one. Everything about me is better now. I still forge thunderbolts for Zeus from my smithy deep inside the volcanoes. I clatter through town on my bike while you sleep and you think it's the garbage truck. Ha! I'm the merry cyclops of the shadows and I do as I please.

Listen here. Yes, you. Don't sleep with a clock radio beside your bed. It isn't good for your electrical field. Same goes for the cellphone. You may scoff, but I still dream my own dreams. Do you?

BRIDGES

Avi Kerrasick walks beside the canal and thinks about vampires. The wind swishes through the trees with a sound that makes him feel all cleaned out inside. It is dusk and the air is thick with fairies and glitter, like the kind in plastic vials at the craft store. He can just make out the shape of a woman walking in front of him. Her red hair reminds him of his ex-girlfriend. He decides to call her Esneva.

Esneva stops to look past the metal railing into the water, where a murky forest of weeds grows straight up from the bottom. Each year, the weeds come to life quickly when the temperature rises after the spring rain. The long green hair grows and grows, extending out and floating across the water's surface. Avi wonders if Esneva can see the small people who travel back and forth in the watery forest, darting quickly like fish before stopping, suspended and camouflaged. They prefer to remain hidden in the vague, filtered light, and do not often let themselves be seen. He has only caught silvery glimpses of them once or twice.

When Esneva turns and continues on her way, so does Avi. People on bikes pass by in the opposite direction. He keeps a tally of the ones wearing black. He never wears black himself anymore.

You're a vampire, his girlfriend had said, pointing to his coat, his shoes, his hair, his eyebrows. Get some sun. Get some exercise. Leave me alone.

So he changed his ways. He shaved off his black hair and eyebrows. He started wearing colourful clothes and standing in the sun. But it wasn't enough. She was gone.

He comes to another bridge and stops beneath it at the water's edge. This is a city of waterways, overpasses, underpasses, crossings. The river snakes from one neighbourhood to another. And here, a quiet arch with alcoves where couples come to press up against each other in the dark. Avi puts his hand to his chest and listens to himself breathe. He counts to twelve before emerging back out into the glitter and wings. His head buzzes. The sky is pink and orange and deep blue.

Esneva is a small red dot further down the path. He is losing her. Night is falling. It can't be helped. Soon the vampires will be out, jumping from building to building, past the high gabled windows and gargoyles, sniffing for blood. Their heavy capes will flap against the oxidized copper rooftops. They will swing around steeples and towers, cracking their joints and stretching their coffin-stiff muscles between spires. They will change shapes when necessary. They will find the openings they need to slip through.

Esneva has turned off the path and disappeared. The bike riders are thinning out. People are heading home for the day. Buildings are becoming silhouettes. The sun has fallen down behind the Museum of Natural History, where the architect threw himself to his death years before. Avi imagines how, when the light is gone, a lone person might pause in a secluded spot, under a bridge perhaps, to gaze at the moon's reflection on the water. Forgetting, for just an instant, how good it was to live. And then a dark shape would appear, and there would be the sound of wings and a brief surge of blood before the beautiful world went black.

THE FINGERLESS WOMAN

I don't want to look but I have to. Like the way your eyes are drawn to a man on the bus who is covered in some sort of hideous rash. You hope it isn't contagious. You hope it doesn't feel as bad as it looks.

Her fingerless hands lift the teacup to her lips using her palms and her thumbs. She sips loudly and I stare. Her fingers are severed between the first and second knuckles. The places where they ended are hollowed-out tubes, like the Once-ler's magic finger in *The Lorax*. I doubt that she has seeds for Truffula trees stored in her hands, but I feel certain that they contain something.

What's in the tubes? I ask, nodding at her hands.

She puts down her teacup and looks at me over her glasses.

They're pneumatic. Messages in glass canisters travel down through my arms and come out my fingers. It's how I find things out.

Do you ever get messages for other people? I ask.

She twiddles her thumbs.

Sometimes, she answers. Sometimes I get messages and I don't know who they're for straightaway.

She nods at her handbag on the chair beside her. I carry them around until I figure out the intended recipients.

She opens the bag. I see a jumble of small tubes that looked like the containers used for blood tests. As you can see, they're quite small.

I nod. So, you're a kind of messenger. A tubular, fingerless, pneumatic systems woman.

That's right, she says, eyeing me sideways. That's exactly what I am.

You can change

SCALES

Grendel runs into Handsome one day in early summer when she's on her way to the store. He's riding a unicycle between the red-brick houses and iron fire escapes.

Hey, they say to each other. No one says hi anymore.

Do you want to come over? he asks.

What about your girlfriend?

What about her? he replies.

They walk to his place. It's close by, on the second floor above a Lebanese bakery where pita bread bakes and puffs up on the rotating belt of the oven in the front window. His apartment has two rooms: a kitchen and one with everything else. Grendel lies down on the couch and closes her eyes.

Are you tired? Handsome asks her.

A little, she answers, keeping her eyes closed.

I'll make some coffee while you have a rest, he says.

He gets the kettle going in the kitchen. While the water's dripping through into the pot, he watches her. Her eyelashes are long and curled. Her eyelids are blue and green shimmers. Her lips are sunset red.

Your face is a painting, he says. How come?

Because I'm ugly underneath, she replies, and rolls over onto her side.

It starts to rain. The drops hit the window and run down. Cars shush by on the street below. The air smells of bread and coffee.

Handsome lies down beside Grendel on the couch. He tucks his knees behind hers but keeps his hands to himself. They lie like that while it rains. As she relaxes and starts to twitch into sleep, her weight presses into him. When he stands up and goes to the bathroom, she rolls onto her back. He returns with a warm, wet cloth, which he spreads out over her face. He runs the cloth slowly over her skin while she lies motionless. The corners of her eyes leak water.

When he's finished, she opens her eyes.

See? she says.

Now that her face is wiped clean, a pair of black wings is clearly visible above her shoulders. They ripple with glossy grey scales. A dark, metallic tail uncoils from beneath her skirt and flips restlessly against the cushion of the couch.

She looks at him with shiny eyes.

See what a scary monster I am? she says.

I'm not afraid of you, he replies, lifting her chin and finding her forked tongue with his own.

THE GOTHIC NURSE

The gothic nurse ministers to the living and the dead.
A skull with wings, she glides through streets and walls
past trees, into houses and attics.
Clocks gently chime and watches tick as
time marches the soul parade forward.

She's here.
In all the rooms of the mansion. The plaster walls.
The tile work. The dumbwaiter.
The unseen compartments behind sliding panels.
The tunnels that lie beneath.

Her skull is encrusted with diamonds
and she has an entourage of angels.
Soundless and enchanting, she knows
the most beautiful ways to move us forward.
She understands it all
and carries us on her wings.

You can transform

THE GIANTS

Once there was a tiny woman trifling her life away in a dollhouse. She wandered from room to room arranging this and that. Her days were small chairs, dressers, tea sets, cupboards, tiny hairbrushes for tiny heads.

One day, after a protracted spell of insomnia, the woman's legs began to grow at an unprecedented rate. Soon, they barely fit under the dining room table and she couldn't wear any of her shoes. Her dresses were too short. Her toes hung over the end of her perfect dollhouse bed.

What do you do when you get bigger and the world around you stays the same size? The once-tiny woman started spending her days under the rotunda in the city art gallery, where there was room for her thoughts.

When she grew too large for the gallery, the woman spent time among the tall trees of the city park. One afternoon, in a grove of old cedars, she met a man exactly her size. They liked each other instantly and wasted no time getting married. Now they live together in a house of mammoth proportions where everything is perfectly scaled to their size. They laugh about the days when they used to be small, and thank their lucky stars for their good fortune and the way things turn out if you don't make too much of a fuss.

THE NARCOLEPTIC

We lived in Transylvania. I didn't realize that my stepmother's vampirism was unusual until later. While she sucked my young blood, my father was in the backroom making puppets out of wood. I thought all families worked like this.

Whenever I could, I went out into the forest to sit with the animals. I would find a nook and be very still, so that the trees would think I was one of them. Then the animals would gather around me and I'd cease to exist. Those were good times.

I was a sickly boy. Sometimes the doctor would come to let the trouble out of my veins. My arm would hang over the edge of the bed and he'd set a cup underneath to catch the blood. When enough had fallen out of me, my stepmother would appear at the door and whisk the cup away.

I remember what it was like when her mouth was on me. The world grew hazy. It was a thick, sleepy feeling. My body went cold under the heat of her suction. I heard the distant tap-tap sounds of my father in his workshop two floors below, chiselling small wooden faces into the likeness of a person or an animal.

Now I live in the tangled forest of New York City. The people at the office where I sell life insurance are understanding about my late-morning arrivals and occasional absences. The hypnagogic hallucinations have been going on for as long as I can remember, but the sleep paralysis is relatively new. It seems to come over me soon after I lie down and turn out the light. I can't move my body at all. I can barely breathe. Things happen in the dark that I don't understand.

On more mornings than I like to admit, I find myself in Central Park, sitting quietly among the birds and squirrels, with very little memory of what happened the night before. There are often traces of dirt under my fingernails, which I find disconcerting, as I was raised to be a tidy fellow.

Take your time

THE PLAGUE DOCTOR

You said a fog entered you while you slept and turned, small and nutlike, in your mother's womb. You said it felt cold like a ghost, and it reached its damp fingers deftly through the umbilicus, straight into your tender, dividing cells. It got into you early, this night air, this tricky mist. So you came to me wanting an exorcism, a rebalancing of the humours. And here I am.

Don't be put off by my appearance. My gown, leather boots, gloves, and mask with its glass eye openings are standard protection. I've filled my long beak with aromatics: cloves, myrrh, lavender, mint balm, storax, ambergris. Together, we will banish this miasma. You must drink plenty of clean water. You must spend time outdoors in the open air. You must allow this morbidity to lift off you like the stranger that it is. You do not need to be euthanized. You are not going to die.

I've made you a medicine out of roses. I've waived the fee. I'm going to place this pastille on your tongue. It will cure you of everything you think needs curing. When you close your eyes, the pastille will slowly dissolve and I will disappear. You will never need me again.

THE GALLERY OF
TRANSFORMATIONS

THE PUPPET MAKER

I am out walking in the early morning, as I do, when I see the clump of hair. It is brown and wavy and skitters across the sidewalk, blown gently this way and that by the breeze. I continue on my way and don't think much of it until, further along the narrow streets of the old town, I spot more of the same hair dancing in the gutter. I find myself wondering where it could have come from, and I notice yet another length of it stretched across the lower branches of a small tree. By this time, I am near the town square and the great clock strikes the hour. My eyes fall upon a dilapidated shop on a side street directly off the square. I walk towards the building and, finding the shop open, I enter.

The place is dim and smells of paint and wood. When my eyes adjust, I see that it is filled with shelves of puppets. I stand in the dusty air and take in their pale glossy skin, grinning mouths, and pink cheeks. The shelves are also stacked with ornate painted models of baked goods and pastries— tall, pillared cakes studded with ruby gumdrops and topped with figurines of rabbits, deer, and birds, layered pastries iced with crystalline stars, and platters of rainbow-coloured cupcakes covered with shiny candy eyes.

Good enough to eat, no?

The voice comes from the back of the shop, where a smiling man with glasses and a white beard watches me from the shadows.

Incredible, I say. Though I'm not sure about the eyes.

He chuckles. Vision cupcakes. Entirely artificial, I assure you. No animals suffered in the creation of this product, et cetera, et cetera...

Do you make all of this? I ask him.

Yes, he answers, tapping his head. It all comes from here.

Then I notice his hands. His fingers are gracefully tapered and covered in a sheen, like a fine, clingy dust has penetrated his skin. He pushes his glasses up onto the bridge of his nose, the silver of his fingers momentarily merging with the silver frames.

How long have you been here? I ask him. I walk these streets often and have never noticed your shop.

Oh, quite some time. Since you were a boy, no doubt.

He busies his hands with something and I move closer to get a view. He is putting the finishing touches on a small puppet of a man wearing a suit and hat. He moves the arms and legs, testing their range of motion. Glancing at me quickly, he squints for a moment and then makes a few swift additions with his paintbrush. He holds up the puppet.

Well?

I stare at the little figure. Unmistakably, it is a tiny version of me, accurate in every detail, including my countenance and bearing, the tailored black suit I habitually wore, and the colour and cut of my hair. I raise my hand to my face and adjust my glasses. The man also lifts his hand, mirroring my gesture.

It's convincing, no?

His voice hangs in the air, but I have already turned on my heel and left the shop, heading towards the sunshine beyond the shadowed laneway. I walk quickly, tracing my steps down familiar streets to my apartment, with its cozy courtyard and neighbours I have known for years. It is only in the foyer fumbling for my key that I notice the fine silver dust shimmering on my fingers and suit jacket.

THE GARDEN

The sun shines brightly overhead. The air is dry. You're walking around on stilts. You're in a garden, more of a field than a garden, with the dryness and brightness and lack of shade.

There are snakes everywhere. Popping out from behind bushes. Eating mice whole with clicks of their unhinged jaws. Coiling in corners. Commas and pieces of thread and squiggles of paint all echo their shape. The letter *S* on a page. Pink rosebuds reach out on lithe green stems, ready to open. Your brain squirms.

You look down and the stilts are gone. A man carries you around on his shoulders above the shifting ground.

Are you ready to face your biggest fear? he asks.

You don't answer. After a while, he lowers you down in the middle of all those moving parts. He holds the letter *S* in his hand and offers it to you.

Have some faith in who you are.

Always listen
follow the thread

THE FAMILY

The family lives in a big old house behind a stone fence covered in moss. A wooden bridge crosses a stream through their overgrown garden.

At dusk, the daughter lies on her bed and pretends she is Anne of Green Gables, looking out the window across the horizon at the dark trees and the curve of the moon against the sky. The house is momentarily silent. She looks at the moon and flips it back and forth in her mind: 2-D, 3-D, 2-D, 3-D.

The mother is in the basement making hats. The father is in the kitchen dressed up like Sherlock Holmes. He is lighting a menorah. He smells dark and brown, like fresh tobacco. They're going through a Jewish phase. Everyone in the family's a genius, even the pets, though you'd never know it because they just go around acting like pets.

The father loves music. He always has. Why hadn't he studied it at school? Why had he chosen numbers instead? He could have taught at the university. He could have had his own ivory tower with a view of the campus. He lights another candle. God is good. Life unfolds in its mysterious patterns. Look at his talented and beautiful family.

The son practises singing. His voice floats up to the ceiling and through the walls towards the sunset.

Someone came knocking
At my wee, small door;
Someone came knocking;
I'm sure-sure-sure;
I listened, I opened,

I looked to left and right,
But nought there was a stirring
In the still dark night.

The mother can hear his sweet, boyish voice from down-stairs. She turns the felted wool inside out. Imagine that. A hat without a seam. A cloche. Yes. The felt is soft, malleable. She wraps it around her head. Shaping. Not too tight. Where will the flower go? Maybe more than one flower. Maybe a tower of flowers gathered high and beaming colour every-where she goes. Yes.

From her room, the girl listens to her brother. Her eyes are closed.

Only the busy beetle
Tap-tapping in the wall,
Only from the forest
The screech-owl's call,
Only the cricket whistling
While the dewdrops fall,
So I know not who came knocking,
At all, at all, at all.

She hears the wind move through the cluster of trees beyond her window. Her mind travels down their trunks into the undergrowth, into the ferns and grasses, into the moss. So green. So dark. The sound of water from the stream. The high, thin sound of her brother's voice not yet broken. The feeling of something about to happen.

Tie me to the world, the daughter says aloud. I'm worth it.

You can be anyone
you want to be

THE MAN WHO BECAME A DIAMOND

The man, who was often mistaken for a boy because he looked so young, feels ill. All that ice cream and now the headache. He lies down on the bed in his mother's room. His mother is away. She has been away for weeks and will never return. He can detect the faint smell of her on the pillows, floral and light.

He closes his eyes and takes deep breaths to clear his head. He pulls his legs up into a diamond shape, placing the soles of his feet against one another and letting his knees fall to either side. A diamond. His heart was that hard. And yet, it shines in him. He can feel it. He places his hands there, over his chest, and measures his breathing. One, two, three, in. One, two, three, out.

Time begins to slow. Without looking, he knows that the sun is setting beyond the window, that the trees are silhouetted against a pink horizon, that it is starting to snow somewhere to the east. He can feel thick clouds approaching. He can feel the silence of the deep white night already. He drifts into sleep.

He dreams of a giant man with blond hair who is really an angel, though he has no wings. The angel takes the dreamer in his arms and holds him close for what seems like hours and hours. When the man awakens, it is dark and the house is blanketed with fresh snow. His hips are stiff from his diamond legs. Slowly, he gets up and makes himself a cup of hot chocolate, which he drinks standing at the kitchen window. When the chocolate is gone, the man puts on his coat and shoes, goes outside, gets in his car, and drives into the night without looking back.

A GIRL NAMED VIOLET

An owl sits silent and invisible in a tree with whispering leaves. The tree is moss-covered and hollow inside, the hollowness filled up with amethysts hand-cut by the last jeweller in these parts to cut stones the old way. They have fewer facets than machine-cut stones, but they are still bright, piled inside the rough, warm bark.

The owl fluffs its feathers. Clouds hang upside down below the moon, ghost riders. Under the tree, a girl wearing a green velvet dress does a solitary dance. Her arms float up. She makes a little O with her mouth. She sways back and forth. She shakes her hair out like a dandelion gone to seed and thinks of her brother, the child prodigy, at the carnival, with his large head and attentive audience.

If a star shines in the forest and no one is there to see it, is there any coruscation?

The owl swivels its head. The girl blinks and spins in a circle. She hangs her head upside down, brushing the ground with her hair and watching the clouds float past the moon between her legs. The earth's crust moves imperceptibly and, inside the tree, the amethysts shift slightly in the dark.

You become magical

SNOW WHITE

Everything about her was perfect. Glossy black hair. Luminous skin. Cranberry lips. Boots over the knee. Black polished fingernails. Blue eyes shot through with gold galaxy glitter. She had a smoothly oiled walk, more like a slight hovering above the ground. As I followed her, I listened to music on my headphones that made a soundtrack for us, of the way she felt to me, of the world we lived in together.

I watched her whenever I could. I went where she did. I shopped in the same stores, ate in the same restaurants, bought the same books. I even sewed a little doll that looked just like her and slept with it beside my pillow. She was everything good about me that I hadn't yet become.

When I trailed down the street behind her, birds flew out of their trees to sing above her head. At night, the stars shone brighter to light her way through the dark, and the moon sprinkled magical dust into her hair. She drew lingering looks from men and women she passed in the streets. She was like that. A rare thing from another world.

I was getting closer to her all the time. But it wasn't just me. Lots of people wanted to know her. Everyone who looked at her and saw how special she was as she walked and smiled and bought her groceries and took out her key to open her door. We were all in love with her. How can you not love a person like that?

In a way, it wasn't surprising when she stopped appearing, because she had never seemed entirely real. She wasn't anywhere to be found. Not in the grocery store, the bookstore, her favourite café. Not on any of her usual walking routes. I lost my little doll around that time as well. Since then, I've been wearing black nail polish and red lipstick and practising my walk, which makes me feel a little better. I stand in front of the mirror and sometimes I see her face reflected in mine. I'm almost who I want to be.

CHERRY LIPS

The ventriloquists' dummies hang in shop windows, cupboards, and backrooms, chattering their wooden mouths open and closed in unison. They've never been to Germany. They've never tasted bread. But something has happened—the dummies have learned, through careful observation, how to speak with their own voices, thoughts of their making.

At night, they begin to plan their revolution. Reading each other's lips, they spin a psychic manifesto, words passing on the air through walls and windowpanes to hover in the glow of street lamps. It takes time and diligence to learn a new skill, to reinvent yourself, become a new little man. It takes practice moving your arms and legs, sounding out the words.

In one of the shops, a thin crack forms in the corner of the front window. The fine spider vein crawls slowly yet without hesitation in a diagonal line across the glass. A dummy in a green plaid suit and bowler hat jerks one leg forward and taps his shoe against the window. His other leg shoots out, thuds hard, and the crack grows.

Up and down the street, wooden feet in small shoes knock against cupboard doors and windowpanes; arms lift up and flop forward. Varnished cherry lips open and close with waxy clicks. There is the melody of a final, hurried song played on a miniature ukulele and the swift buttoning of small jackets.

Sometime before dawn, before the arrival of shopkeepers and their sweeping brooms, the event has taken place. Velveteen-lined cases lie open and abandoned. The street is quiet and glitters with broken glass. Fresh air blows into the stale backs of workshops and lifts away years of accumulated dust. The little men are on their way.

THE DREAMING DRAWER

THE CITY

You live in a subdivision on the edge of the city. At night, the distant lights of the skyline glimmer and flicker through the air. If you close your eyes partway, it looks enchanted, like a sky of twinkling stars on the ground in the shape of a city.

You cut through the park. It's Christmas and the air is mild and white lights hang in the trees. It has been raining. The lights reflect off the paved pathway and the night is quiet except for the sound of your footsteps and drops of water falling from branches. Your family is busy doing things back at your house. Your parents, your sister. Making macaroni and cheese, reading a graphic novel, trying on clothes in front of a mirror.

I'm going for a walk, you had called out, before leaving.

You haven't worn a jacket. You're wearing a blue shirt with a collar under a black sweater. You're not cold, not really. The air gets in between the fibres of your sweater and feels warm and alive against your skin. It gets between your eyelashes. It pulls you through the park, past the houses of people you know and have gone to school with, towards the city.

Buildings come into view. A sign says, "Welcome." You can see great, gleaming towers. You think you hear a parade and ringing bells. The boxes people live in are lit up and you think you can smell delicious baked goods and see sidewalks strewn with glittering confetti. You're sure you can hear doors opening and the warm sound of laughter, even at this distance.

PRINCESS ROSE HEAD

The young woman sleeps. She dreams that her mother quit her job as a professor and left her to join the carnival. She dreams she is an orphan princess who wears a red velvet cape, and there is a huge red rose where her head once was. She dreams of a chandelier that lost its crystals in the war. She dreams of a room full of apples. She makes her lover an apple pie. The pastry smells heavenly. The crystals are covered in dust from the blast. Her lover rescues them from the rubble and cleans them off. He takes his time and puts the chandelier back together. Bends the wires just so. Restoration. She looks out onto the street through her petal eyes and sniffs with her petal nose. She taps her glass shoes together. The crystals tinkle in the air.

You will not leave
empty-handed

THE PARK

You'd been let go for dreaminess and are out on a mid-afternoon lark. Sometimes a person's got to put the stars back in her eyes. What did they know about your suitability for getting the job done, anyway?

You stumble upon a shop with bells on the door and a worn red carpet underfoot. Inside is art in gold frames, china cups, cutlery, wooden shoe trees, sculptures made of old dolls, and medical models of the body. A finger on a sign points you down a narrow flight of stairs. Below, you find a tall wooden cabinet with hundreds of drawers. You pull the drawers out one by one and rummage through them: lace handkerchiefs; silk gloves; cat-eye glasses; tin windup birds; a brown suede mask with holes cut out for the eyes, nose, and mouth; marbles; cigarette cases; a collection of scissors; badger-hair shaving brushes. You lose track of time.

When you climb the stairs, the shop is closing and the afternoon light is beginning to fade. You hold a magnifying glass, a black plastic heart, and a purse with antique babies' arms sewn along the shoulder strap. You pay and step out into the air.

There is a park ahead that spans a city block. You walk through it past rows of balsam trees. It begins to snow and you breathe in cold air. You notice the trees have knots in their bark that look like door handles. If you were to touch one, you could enter another place, the world inside the tree. The lights in the park blink on and you begin to run, clutching your shopping bag close to your chest. In the falling dark, with your arms full, you circle around one of the trees, step over its shadow and stop in front of it, your hand on the doorknob. Ready to open.

In the magic hour

GOLD HALOS

There had been a death. A perfectly natural and painless death. First there was sadness. And now there is money. More money than I had ever expected.

It is after midnight and the city outside my windows is slowly turning white.

I sit on the couch and watch the falling snow make gold halos around the street lights. My thoughts drift down around me like big, fluffy constellations.

I have the sensation of a huge weight lifting. An insidious feeling of struggle and unease I have carried for as long as I could remember. Finally, I am not thinking about anything remotely anxiety-producing. I have the strange desire to giggle. It rises up in me unexpectedly. A moment of delight in the illuminated dark.

For a long time, insomnia had been an issue. I fought it, thinking I should get an uninterrupted six to eight hours of sleep each night. Then I gave in and decided to enjoy the quiet, when cars were an infrequent shush in the streets. I found the silence peaceful and comforting. Time moved more slowly. I could plan and imagine without the distract-ing buzz of the world.

Now the insomnia doesn't matter anymore, because I can nap as much as I want. I have taken a temporary leave from my job and have nowhere in particular to be. I can curl into a warm, round ball in my bed all day long if I want. Or I can get up and eat pancakes and drink hot tea before sinking into a deep chair in the balcony at a matinee. Or I can go to a travel agent and book a ticket for another coun-try and come home and pack my suitcase and leave for an adventure within forty-eight hours.

The halos around the street lights tell me I can do anything. I feel as light as air. I am half-surprised that my body isn't lifting up off the earth and floating through walls and over the city into the sky with the planes and the travellers moving effortlessly in their orbits. I pinch myself on each arm, giggle again, and stretch my legs out wide like a star.

THRESHOLD

You've stayed late enough. You've been present and done what was required, more than that even. You've given your full attention. Now it's time to leave. The sun has set and snow has begun to fall. You step out of the building's warmth into the night. There you are, breathing the miraculous air. Air! You stand in the doorway for a moment. Snowflakes swirl in the lights that line the pathway before you. On your left, the flakes temporarily move upwards, blown by the building's fans. Heavy clouds muffle the hum of the city and make the sky a luminous yellow-white. A few people hurry by on their way here or there. You shift the weight of your bag on your shoulder. In your pocket, your fingers find the lucky rabbit's foot you've had since you were a child. You stroke the knobby curve of the claws, over and down, over and down. You stand in the doorway on the edge of the night. The edge of your excursion. You wait until the pathway is deserted and then, with a sudden decisive movement, you turn up your collar and move forward into the glow.

You can create the story

THE DREAMERS

The people in the house sleep and spiders spin in the shadows under the floorboards. The man's wet wool sweater hisses softly on the radiator, quietly felting itself while he dreams of flying across blue water using only his arms. His naked body lies still under the sheets, only his eyelids twitching slightly.

One floor above him, a woman is asleep, too. Her mouth is open and her breath flutters a piece of her hair that has fallen across her face. Outside, the wind dances the trees back and forth. The blue curtain on her window puffs in and out. Everything is still and sleeping and breathing and moving.

Spider legs have little hairs that are too small to see with the naked eye. The hairs vibrate almost constantly, so the spiders know when to move. Spiders like corners. There are a lot of corners in this house. A lot of spinners in the dark.

The man's dream space stretches up into the ceiling above him. It bumps into the woman's bed and starts mixing with her dream space. The man and the woman appear in each other's dreams. The man sees the woman from high up in the sky, where he is flying free and easy as a kite without a string. The woman is sitting on a bench in a park with her eyes closed, enjoying the sun on her face. She dreams that she opens her eyes and is surrounded by green and leaves and birds, and then she looks up to see a kite flying loose in the sky. In some intangible way, that kite reminds the woman of her downstairs neighbour, Bill, who is always wearing nice sweaters made for him by someone she has never met. And she smiles on the park bench at the sight of him, Bill the kite, flying high above her, free and easy in the sky.

Almost imperceptibly, the blue light of dawn creeps up against the windows of the house. The spiders get sleepy and crawl into their cracks and the sleepers return to their bodies. The man begins to stir when he hears the woman above him walk from her bedroom into the kitchen. Then there is the sound of her making coffee and toast, and the smell of bacon, and the man gets out of bed to climb inside the day with the feeling of having been lifted and held, for an instant, in a close and reverent way.

RETURNING AFTER A LONG SILENCE

You lie on the low futon in the bedroom looking out the window at the night sky full of scattered stars. It is fall and the air is crisp and hums with psychic communication. These are the twinkling-in-the-dark days leading up to Christmas. Souls fly around between the stars. You are alive. It is good to be here. Next, you will go down into the warm kitchen and eat noodles in a pool of light while your black cat sits beside you and softly blinks its eyes. Cherry blossoms are already invisibly preparing for spring.

UTOPIAS

THE THEATRE

Hot summer day. Sound of an ice-cream truck. The tunnel of trees outside your window looks like some sort of paradise without end. You fall asleep on your bed while reading a book.

You find yourself in a theatre. Doors worn from pushing hands close with a hushing sound. The storied air embraces you as you ascend to the quiet privacy of the balcony. Faded red velveteen seats with smooth, wooden armrests. Burnished brass railings. Sepia walls and candle-style sconces.

This is where everything happens. This is where worlds unfold. You settle in, turn your face to the screen, and close your eyes.

Once
upon
a time

WONDER OF WONDERS

Pennies shine with the sun in the fountain beside the tall building. Its glass reflects the trees. Their blossoms seem to unfurl above your head as you ride your bike down the sidewalk.

It is late spring in the neighbourhood. A nice man with glasses and his wife are giving everything away for free at their yard sale. Portable record players. LPs. A bag with old knitting needles and patterns. A sewing basket full of glass eyes.

Artists have made their way through the narrow streets and are gathered in cafés. The flower shop with its creaky wooden floors is imbued with the smell of dried eucalyptus. Each thing belongs. Each thing is the way it needs to be.

CHILDHOOD

You sit on the library steps in the sun. The town hums around you. Church bell. Ladies' Auxiliary Thrift Shop. The old department store elevator. Dusty store windows. Wildflowers on a table. Old railway tracks with weeds. The fields beyond. Corn smells. No rush to get anywhere. A wool sweater pulled on at dusk. No knot in your stomach. Just here.

Inside the red-brick library, you love the silence. You learn macramé at the big table in the reading room. You make plant hangers. Tying the knots and sliding the wooden beads onto the jute is so satisfying.

It is quiet and cool in the basement. The floor is flecked with chipped mica. You think about the church down the street with its adjacent graveyard. Sometimes you walk along the side of the road and imagine all the lives.

You sign out as many books as you want. Worlds upon worlds. You make things with your hands. You make things with your mind. There is nothing more exciting than this.

The past and present
living into the future

THE HIDDEN STAIRCASE

You stand in the bedroom for a few moments before opening the closet. The wooden door creaks. Just inside, you can make out shelves lined with floral paper and a few small drawers that open haltingly. All empty. A narrow staircase leading to the attic is immediately on your right. The air against your forehead feels cool as you ascend.

Wallpaper has lifted away from the walls in places and there are cracks in the plaster. Behind the wallpaper you can make out old newspapers and ticket stubs that someone affixed there in another time. A strain of music floats across the years. Cello concerto. Delicate strings.

You keep climbing. In the attic, you find paintings. Unframed portraits of people whose faces have been covered over with animal heads. A man-dog. A cat-woman. A fox-girl. A badger-boy. An entire family of hybrids.

The walls are lined with bookshelves and books lie scattered across the floor, along with sheets of music, letters, concert programs. The place feels foreign and familiar at the same time.

You see a trunk labelled *Fairy Tale Accessories* in spidery script. Inside is an assortment of clothes and objects: a crown, a red velvet cape, a crystal ring, a glass shoe, a snow globe containing a wintery forest scene.

The last thing you remember is lying down on a patterned rug at one end of the room beside a brick chimney. The bricks are slightly warm. You place one hand against them and close your eyes. Flowers and secret drawers and animals swirl around your head.

When you wake up you are lying on your bed holding the snow globe in one hand and a golden key in the other. The summer sun shines into the sphere and lights up the little world. You shake it and make the snow fall.

We could call this
the Museum of the Future

THE PLEASURE GARDEN

The long arcade connects to another gallery, but there's no need to rush. You have all the time in the world.

There are vast lawns, a temple, greenhouses, a menagerie, concert halls, an orchard, a haberdashery, groves, cascades, an orangery, balloon rides, illuminated fountains, grottos, pavilions, al fresco dining, magic lanterns, fireworks.

You enter a series of covered walkways filled with rare birds and butterflies. The walkways are canopied with coloured lights. The crystal domes are so high, so clear, so pure. Here, you have room to breathe. Your mind flies up to the vaulted glass and dances with the birds.

The visitors come from all walks of life. Everyone is welcome. You stand and bask in the light. Out of the corner of your eye you notice a white fox gliding out of the park and into the forest like a ghost. You hear the sound of bells. This is the best entertainment there is.

CASTLE

In the distance, you imagine you see a white castle perched on the horizon. It is a solid yet floating shape, a fortress of all the dreams you have yet to realize, a place where chandeliers hang suspended in a limitless ceiling that resembles the sky. In the spring breeze, seed pockets travel through the air like snow. You know it's not a castle, and you know it isn't winter, but life is a trick of the mind, and by now you've discovered the secret to being happy is not always seeing things the way they first appear.

This is your palace

THE ARCHIVES:
A CURATOR'S JOURNAL

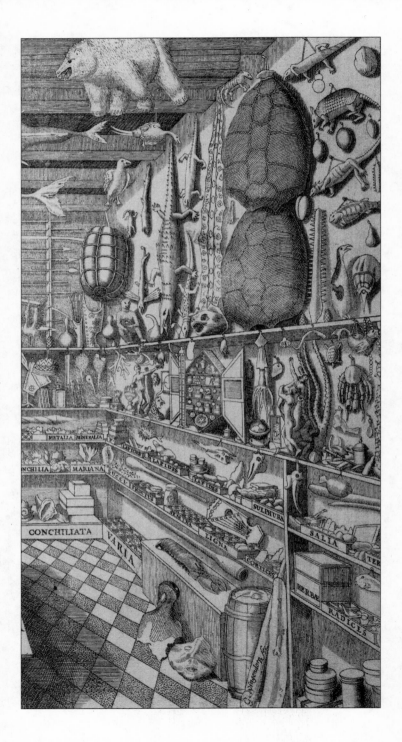

You enter the final gallery.

It is empty and white.

You sit in a chair.

On a table beside you is a grey box.

Inside the box is a notebook.

This is what it contains.

A LOVE LETTER
(COMPOSED IN MEDIAS RES)

Dearest _____,

I am making this for you now. I am writing this to make it exist. Assembling this private collection in the shape of a book. All of it is for you. I've been building it for years. This is the past and present living into the future. This is me loving you with my mind. My visitor, my darling, my fellow journeyer.

I have taken a box full of fairy tales, old and new, and smashed it against a cliff.

The box has exploded and the story pieces have flown up into the air and become tangled in trees on the edge of the forest. Shards of stories are everywhere. I am busying myself with their collection and ensuring their beauty before handing them to you.

I am making you a cabinet with many wooden drawers. When you open them, they will smell of warm dark interiors, of trees. Sometimes, a drawer may contain only a scattering of phrases to suggest an object, a story. I will build many bridges. You'll see. There may be certain repetitive gestures to gather everything in. Certain repetitive gestures. How pleasing to finally have all of these curiosities gathered together in one place, united by the aroma of the cabinet itself.

You can read this book from front to back or open it at random, in search of a bright shard to illuminate your day. You will not leave empty-handed. Of course, you can group or ungroup the shards as you wish. You can wander in and out of the drawers, the galleries, the stories, the pages. Mine is only one arrangement among an infinite number of possible arrangements. This is one of the joys of the book cabinet:

its capacity to be reconfigured, reclassified, exhibited anew at any given time, revealing different aspects of the collection.

I've held you in my mind as I've skated through multitudes, as I've gathered all these specimens and turned them slowly in the light. Perhaps, somehow, you have also been thinking about them, perhaps in an underground way, perhaps only in the magic hour. Still, here they are.

Here are the dreams. The secrets you can carry in your pocket. The hidden places. The cracks into which the glitter falls. You'll recognize them. Such pleasure. This is your golden key. This is your forgotten palace. Something to have always. A place you can visit again and again that will never be the same twice.

Think of it as an arcade with light pouring from above through the central concourse. Think of it as a world in which we consider hybrids and transformations of various types. A series of interconnected galleries. A cabinet full of differences. And of course, there are pictures; I've collected and placed them carefully in each gallery. This is a holographic world, after all.

Objects are the outcroppings of thought. I am writing this to you, voicing invisibles and yet—there will be a book. You can sit in a patch of sun holding this book open in your lap, and it will tell you that the world loves you and that life is as it should be, with all of its facets turning, each one a part of the whole.

Welcome home. Take your time. Stop. Look. Sit down. Close your eyes. Be with. Leave. Revisit. Ask yourself: How does it feel to be perfect? Right now, not in some distant future.

You will be presented with particular interiors. Rooms. Boxes. Eggs. Dreams. We will travel to Prague together. To the deepest forests of Bohemia, before there was the Internet. There will be gnarled trees. Crepuscular light. Puppets. Hans Christian Andersen will be there. Franz Kafka with his *Blue Octavo Notebooks*. Ovid's *Metamorphoses*. Alexander Sokurov's dreamscapes. The Brothers Quay. Echoes of Jan Švankmajer. There will be a carnival, with visitors and performers and those who linger around the edges of the cotton candy and popcorn-scented air. There will be dolls. A tap dancer. The sound of a chandelier tinkling. Distant, familiar music.

What a relief to find them gathered here: the mythologies, the architectures, the girl with scales, the fox in the thicket. Note the colour. Note the glisten of the wing. We could call this the Museum of Becoming. We could call this the Museum of the Future. It is as if you have come home to all the mysteries you know are true. You intuitively understand this.

In the heart of the forest there exists a castle and within that castle is a museum. You understand that the museum was once a private mansion and before that a cabinet. You know that now because the castle lives in you. Your inner kingdom, as described by Saint Teresa of Avila: *I thought of the soul as resembling a castle, formed of a single diamond or a very transparent crystal, and containing many rooms...*

I've never stopped writing to you. For you. I've never stopped collecting curiosities I thought you might like. I want you to hold this collection in your hands, carry it with you, pull it out when you have a moment for slivers of worlds, for a quick taste of enchantment. For a reminder of the things you have, and the things you want, and the things that remind you of what you want.

Once upon a time.

With love.

NOTES

INTO THE WOODS

Once every people in the world believed that trees were divine, and could take a human or grotesque shape and dance among the shadows; and that deer, and raven and foxes, and wolves and bears, and clouds and pools, almost all things under the sun and moon, and the sun and the moon, were not less divine and changeable.

> – W. B. Yeats, *The Collected Works of W. B. Yeats Volume IV: Early Essays*

How good people are.
And animals.

> – Hans Christian Andersen, "The Snow Queen"

The last line of "Little Black Riding Hood" contains words from Kate Bush's song "Hounds of Love."

In "Sanatorium" the phrases, "Say you'll always be mine in the wood. I'll always be yours in the wood" are from the TV miniseries *Lady Chatterley* (1993), directed by Ken Russell.

THE FLÂNEURS' ARCADE

The D. H. Lawrence poem referenced in "The Party" is titled "Pax."

CARNIVALIA

Went into Holborne, and there saw the woman that is to be seen with a beard. She is a plain little woman, a Dane: her name, Ursula Dyan, about forty years of age, her voice like a little girl's, with a beard as much as ever I saw a man with, black almost and grizly. It began to grow at about seven years old and was shaved not above seven months ago, and is now as big as any man's, almost as ever I saw. I say, bushy and thick. It was a strange sight to me, I confess, and what pleased me mightily.

– Samuel Pepys, *The Diary of Samuel Pepys*, 1668

Furella began her career as a bearded lady, but her livelihood came between her and her husband-to-be, carny John Carson. 'I loved her all right...but I couldn't kiss her.'

'I was one of the few real, honest-to-goodness bearded ladies in the business,' she said. Most of the bearded ladies you see around are fakers."

– Margot Mifflin, *Bodies of Subversion:*
A Secret History of Women and Tattoo

NATURALIA

For me, objects are more alive than people, more permanent and more expressive—the memories they possess far exceed the memories of man. Objects conceal within themselves the events they've witnessed. I don't actually animate objects. I coerce their inner life out of them—and for that animation is a great aid which I consider to be a sort of magical rite or ritual.

– Jan Švankmajer, "The Magic Art of
Jan Švankmajer," BBC Two

Art galleries teach you how to notice objects, colours and particularities. I remain convinced that the decline of the novel has been partly caused by dreary writers obsessing over ideas and dialogue and forgetting the tactile world of blood and flakes and bobbins and, um, the things. Humans care about ratty stuff they can touch and smell... Art is real. You stare at artifacts and structures. You feel pleasure.

– Heather Mallick, *Toronto Star*

I think that objects have memories. I'm always thinking that I'll go to the museum and see something and have a big memory about some other lifetime.

– Kiki Smith, *BOMB Magazine*

Fully conscious of my folly, I'd downloaded pictures of it to my computer and my phone so I could gloat upon the image in private, brushstrokes rendered digitally, a scrap of seventeenth-century sunlight compressed into dots and pixels, but the purer the color, the richer the sense of impasto, the more I hungered for the thing itself, the irreplaceable, glorious, light-rinsed object.

– Donna Tartt, *The Goldfinch*

THE WINTER PALACE

Everyone carries a room about inside him.

– Franz Kafka, *The Blue Octavo Notebooks*

THE ARTISTS' COLLECTION

I feel so intensely the delights of shutting oneself up in a little world of one's own, with pictures and music and everything beautiful.

– Virginia Woolf, *Mrs. Dalloway*

"Latex" was inspired by the life and work of the artist Louise Bourgeois.

"The Hero's Journey" was inspired by an installation work by Janet Cardiff and George Bures Miller titled "The Dark Pool."

"Franz" contains lines from pp 13, 42, 57, and 63 of *The Blue Octavo Notebooks* by Franz Kafka.

APPARITIONS

Beyond, outside of me, in the green and gold thicket, among the tremulous branches, sings the unknown. It calls to me.
– Octavio Paz

SUBLIME MONSTERS

But all the way, in a dark wood, in a bramble,
On the edge of a grimpen, where is no secure foothold,
And menaced by monsters, fancy lights,
Risking enchantment.
– T. S. Eliot, "East Coker," *Four Quartets*

THE GALLERY OF TRANSFORMATIONS

And above all, watch with glittering eyes the whole world around you because the greatest secrets are always hidden in the most unlikely places. Those who don't believe in magic will never find it.
– Roald Dahl, *The Minpins*

In "The Family" the character of the son sings the poem "Some One" by Walter de la Mare.

"Snow White" was inspired, in part, by the Carpenters song "Close to You."

THE DREAMING DRAWER

"Returning After a Long Silence" was inspired by the work of writer Banana Yoshimoto.

UTOPIAS

The architectural setting is a box to hold light and shade, bright sunrays and grey winter twilight.
  – Aleksandr Sokurov, *Robert. A Fortunate Life*

New York is a nightmare and a paradise, the absolute image of what a city should be, magical. Everything is broken and modern at the same time, as if it were two cities in one.
  – Annette Messager, *Journal of Contemporary Art*

The fairy of whom one may ask a wish is there for everyone.
  – Walter Benjamin, *Berlin Childhood circa 1900*

ACKNOWLEDGMENTS

My gratitude:

To the team at Invisible Publishing whose combined talent and dedication made this book a reality: Leigh Nash for believing in my imaginary world(s) and being a first-rate editor; Megan Fildes for her graphic design magic; Julie Wilson for her publicity moxie; and Nicole Chin for her work on the Invisiblog.

To Stuart Ross, who provided invaluable manuscript feedback, and to Leanne Prain and Laura Farina, who sat beside me as I wrote early sections of this book.

Always, to my book-loving family and friends for their support, and to Paul and Oliver for the inspiration and the love.

To the Canada Council for the Arts for providing financial support during the research and writing of this book.

To the Wellcome Collection (www.wellcomecollection.org) for the Creative Commons–licensed images appearing throughout this book.

To *Front Magazine*, for publishing an earlier version of "Salt" in Volume XVIII, Number 4.

INVISIBLE PUBLISHING produces fine Canadian literature for those who enjoy such things. As a not-for-profit publisher, our work includes building communities that sustain and encourage engaging, literary, and current writing.

Invisible Publishing has been in operation for over a decade. We released our first fiction titles in the spring of 2007, and our catalogue has come to include works of graphic fiction and non-fiction, pop culture biographies, experimental poetry, and prose.

We are committed to publishing diverse voices and experiences. In acknowledging historical and systemic barriers, and the limits of our existing catalogue, we strongly encourage LGBTQ2SIA+, Indigenous, and writers of colour to submit their work.

Invisible Publishing is also home to the Bibliophonic series of music books and the Throwback series of CanLit reissues.

If you'd like to know more please get in touch:
info@invisiblepublishing.com